In Hollow Lands

In Hollow Lands

Sophie Masson

Hodder
Children's
Books

A division of Hodder Headline Limited

A Catalogue record for this book is available
from the British Library

ISBN 0 340 85442 1

Typeset in Cochin by Avon DataSet Ltd,
Bidford-on-Avon, Warwickshire

Printed and bound in Great Britain by
Clays Ltd, St Ives plc

The paper and board used in this paperback by
Hodder Children's Books are natural recyclable products
made from wood grown in sustainable forests.
The manufacturing processes conform to the environmental
regulations of the country of origin.

Hodder Children's Books
a division of Hodder Headline Limited
338 Euston Road
London NW1 3BH

To Bertrand, who loves the songs of Brittany

Though I am old with wandering
Through hollow lands and hilly lands,
I will find out where she has gone,
And kiss her lips and take her hands;
And walk among long dappled grass,
And pluck till time and times are done,
The silver apples of the moon,
The golden apples of the sun.

The Song of Wandering Aengus
W B Yeats

Part One

One

A long hot summer is always followed by an early, biting winter, so they say. But that year, the wise old sayings about the turning of the seasons looked mighty foolish indeed. Late October, and the twin children of the lord and lady of the manor of Raguenel, Tiphaine and Gromer, could still run around barefoot with their friends, and splash through river shallows without feeling at all cold. The leaves on the trees had barely begun to turn, and there was still a balmy feeling to the wind that was as lovely as it was surprising. No-one on the manor, not even the twins' ancient tutor Dame Viviane, not even the oldest villager, a bent man so old that he looked more like a *duz*, a dwarf, than a man, could remember a year like it.

The clement weather was not universally welcomed, however. Some people, professional glooms all, crept about gazing suspiciously at the cheerful blue sky, and muttered that the end of the world was nigh, and others still prophesied hopefully that 'You mark my words, winter's going to have a real bite to it! It's not right, this weather, it just isn't right! You mark my words, the roads will be full of frozen corpses in a few weeks hence, and the wolves will come back to Stone Wood and wreak havoc on the village!'

Tiphaine and Gromer and their friends didn't waste time worrying about the weather, though. Winter, with everyone solemnly indoors, reading improving works and gossiping by smoky fireplaces, would be here soon enough. They ran and jumped and fished and walked and hunted and danced and sang and generally spun out each hour of extra daylight as long as they possibly could. Nobody tried to stop them: the villagers, busy with the hundred and one preparations farmers must make before winter, looked indulgently on all the children, and did not ask them to do too many chores. Dame Viviane did not attempt to make the twins start the lessons which usually began again in autumn; and their parents, the Viscount and Viscountess Raguenel, were still far away at the Court of the Duke of Brittany. Usually, they returned by mid-October to the manor, but this year they had sent word that they would not return till well after All Saints' Day, if the weather held. If only the weather held! It was like a spell!

And the spell hung over Raguenel that year, like a great warm globe, touching everything with a golden light, a soft mellowness that got into your bones, making the whole manor seem even more beautiful than ever. Raguenel was neither the biggest nor the smallest of the Breton manors, but certainly one of the prettiest and most pleasant. Its lord, the Viscount, was from a junior branch of the great Breton family, the counts of Dinan, though his wife the Viscountess was a foreigner, being French. Like most manors in those days, it was a mixture of farm, orchard, forest holding and riverland. The village, which held about sixty souls or so, was clustered most attractively around the green, where stood the little stone church of Saint Gwenole. There was a small mill and the manor-house, which was large and comfortable, stood not far from the river. The manor was a perfect place for children; the river was neither too swift nor too sluggish, but just right for swimming in, and the wood nearby, known as Stone Wood, because of the stone circle, called Ti-Korriganed, that stood in its centre, was small enough not to be too frightening, but dense enough to be a place of adventure. There were no wolves there any more, or bears; the villagers' incessant battle against marauding wild beasts had finally been won some years back.

Only once in the year was the wood out of bounds: on the eve of All Hallows, or All Saints' Day, October 31st, and the day after that, All Souls' Day, or the Day of the Dead. No-one in their right mind would go there in that time, and especially not on Hallowe'en; for Stone Wood, and especially Ti-Korriganed, was then a place between worlds. Ghosts, demons, witches, the fairies called *korrigans* in Brittany, dwarfs and mary-morgans, as water-spirits were called, and many other kinds of strange beings would emerge into Stone Wood and dance around Ti-Korriganed. If a human being strayed too close, they would get caught up in the dance too, and never return to the human world, or return so changed that they were like walking dead. On those days and evenings, then, people in Raguenel stayed well away from the wood. They went to Mass in the little stone church of Saint Gwenole, which was of the

5

same weathered grey as the megalith, and they prayed for the souls of the dead, and for protection against the other strange denizens of the Otherworld.

Not all of those beings were wicked, of course, or hostile to human beings, but all of them were unpredictable, and thus could be dangerous. It was best to leave them in possession of Stone Wood at that time – for by some kind of unspoken agreement, the otherworlders did not try to invade the village. There were other times – four in all – when the otherworlders could be seen, and not just felt as unseen presences, but it was only on the Day of the Dead that all of the spirits came out together. Normally, the demons and witches and goblins and ghosts kept well away from the korrigans and mary-morgans and dwarfs, for they were, if not always enemies, at least wary of each other.

Tiphaine and Gromer had turned twelve that summer. It was to be their last carefree year as children. They had lived on the manor all their lives and known nothing else, but next year they would both be gone from Raguenel. Gromer would go to a manor near the great forest of Broceliande, where the lord was a friend of his father's. There, he would have to learn the hard tasks that would make him first a squire, then a knight, and eventually lord of Raguenel himself. As to Tiphaine, she would have to learn the life of a lady at the Duke's court, and to attract the attention of some well-born man, for her mother had great plans for her. She certainly did not want her lovely daughter marrying some hedge-squire or Breton-speaking clodhopper! No more bare feet for

Tiphaine, or short, loose shifts; no more flying hair and swims in the river and fits of laughter that showed all her small sharp teeth. She would have to learn to stand tall and straight, and smile politely at gormless suitors and dull officials, and broil on hot summer's days in heavy velvet and silks. Neither Tiphaine nor Gromer would be able to play with the village children in the same wild and free way any more. If it had been left up to their mother, the Viscountess, of course, they would have been packed away from Brittany long ago. Not being from Brittany herself, she was a little shocked at how peasant and knight, lord and villein, seemed to mix much more freely here than in her own country of France, but had agreed reluctantly that the children were to be brought up as country Bretons until their twelfth birthday, on the condition that then they must learn the ways of the Court. The Duke's court was very much influenced by the French court and also that of England, though of course Brittany was independent of both. And so the Viscount had agreed that he would go with his wife every spring and summer to the Duke's court, and keep up the reputation of his family. He knew that his children must eventually learn all the secrets and wiles and traps of the big wide world, though remembering his own happy childhood running wild at Raguenel, he wished that he could keep them there a little longer.

There would be no more Dame Viviane for the twins, either; they would have outgrown the old woman and all she could teach them. Dame Viviane's knowledge was not, or even mostly, out of books; it was country knowledge, of simples and herbs and stars and how to spot a fox's earth and a badger's tracks, and a wealth of stories about korrigans and mary-morgans and all kinds of other beings. She had taught the children to read and write, true, but she spoke French only haltingly, with a strong Breton accent, and did not know anything of the new, fashionable things the Viscountess deemed essential, and so had been told that her services would no longer be required. The Lady of Raguenel would be glad to see the back of her; though Viviane looked like a kind old woman, with a cheerful, appley kind of face, there was something almost cold in the depth of her black eyes when she looked at the Viscountess, which made that lady feel quite chilled.

Nobody knew where Dame Viviane might go afterwards, though the Viscount had, in secret, offered her a little cottage on the edge of the woods, which she had declined with a little smile. Though she was certainly Breton, she was not from Raguenel, for her accent was not of those parts. Perhaps she might return to her original home, or perhaps not. The one thing she would not do was gracefully retire to a convent, as so many older women did. It was not a bad life, a convent, the Viscountess had suggested to her once, but the old woman had looked at her so coldly that she had uncharacteristically shut her mouth on the rest of the sentence. 'Heavens,' she had said crossly to her husband, a little later, 'she looked just like a witch!' The Viscount had laughed a little uneasily; under the Court veneer, he was still very much a Breton, and did not think it at all impossible that Dame Viviane might, indeed, be a witch.

She had come to Raguenel one bright Midsummer

Day twelve years ago, just after the twins' birth, and offered her services as a nurse and tutor. She had said she came from near Broceliande; and indeed, discreet inquiries had revealed she had indeed come from a poor family somewhere on those central lands of Brittany. The Viscount had liked the look of her from the start, and though his wife had not, he had, rather unusually for him, stubbornly insisted on the old woman staying and looking after the children.

You might say Dame Viviane had a certain way with her, even if you did not think she had magical powers. The villagers, strangely, took to her at once: usually they disliked all foreigners. She had even made firm friends with the priest, Sieur Beleg – surely in itself a sign that she was not a witch. And she had indeed proved to be a very good nurse and a thoroughly reliable guardian, freeing the Viscount and Viscountess from worry about the twins at all. But the thought that she would be gone next year was a great relief to the Viscountess, and as for the Viscount, he was still a little uncertain of her, and not sure what to feel about her departure at all. Sometimes, when he stopped to think about it, he felt that since her arrival, things at Raguenel had been very good – the plague, which had devastated many villages around about, had spared Raguenel; the fields had been particularly productive, the fruit trees laden with fat juicy apples and pears and plums, the granaries full. It was almost as if Viviane had been the luck of Raguenel, directing its activities with a benevolent spell. And now there was this brilliant, endless summer, like her last gift. What would happen when she left? The Viscount did not know, and worried about it a little, though he did not say anything to his wife.

But for Tiphaine and Gromer, Viviane's imminent departure aroused quite different feelings. They were not afraid of her or uncomfortable in her presence at all, though they knew not to lack in respect to her. She had been more of a mother and father to them than their parents had been singly or together. She was not stern or fierce with them, only firm, and lively and wise, full of stories that they never tired of listening to. Though she insisted on good manners and respect from them, she also allowed them to run wild all over the manor. Sometimes she came with them for walks in the woods, in the fields, by the river, and then everything would seem to spring alive to the children. The one thing she was neither tolerant nor indulgent about was the prohibition about going to Stone Wood on All Hallows Day, or the Day of the Dead. If anything, she was even stricter about it than the priest, or the villagers. But then, that had never worried them in the least in the past; they had no wish to go near Stone Wood, then, either, and especially not near Ti-Korriganed.

Yes, Tiphaine and Gromer loved Viviane dearly, and would miss her terribly. They did not think that they could have tried to keep her there – for what could children do, when their parents had decreed what must happen? Besides, they knew Viviane herself wanted to go – they had always known she would leave, one day. They did not wonder, either, where Viviane had come from or where she might go to – in a strange way, they felt almost as if without them, she did not exist. They could not imagine her life without them, though, secretly, in recent months, they had begun to imagine life without her. They were growing up. And even if there would be boring and unpleasant things about their new lives, still, it made a change. And there was something exciting about change. There was a new restlessness in them that long summer which sometimes stopped them in the middle of play, a kind of thrill, a quickening of the heart, that was both a little frightening and exciting.

But there was one thing that did bother them both a great deal. Tiphaine and Gromer had never been apart before. Curious and lively and bright, they thought alike and spoke alike and had looked alike until very recently, being fair and delicately pretty and smallish and slender as young children, with surprising black eyes under mops of hair the colour of sunlight. But in recent months, Gromer had begun to get taller and heavier than his sister and now towered above her; his voice had become deeper, his face, though still very handsome, was no longer at all delicate, and fine golden hairs bright as water had begun sprouting on his upper lip. And Tiphaine's body was rounding and filling out; her face, always lovely and lively, had become truly beautiful. They were a very handsome pair, the two of them, but had not yet begun to understand that other people thought so too. They had many gifts, of wit and intelligence and humour, but were not immodest about them, for they had no idea that these were unusual things. They wanted to grow up, and yet did not, if it meant separating. They knew there was no way out of that; they did not even think to try and flout their parents' wishes. Dame Viviane had taught them too well. In any case, there was their secret language, to keep them in touch. Long ago, the twins had discovered that sometimes their minds could speak to each other, without words, even over distances. It could be very useful, at times. Now, it would be comforting as well.

Two

$\mathcal{I}$n another corner of Brittany, many miles away, another twelve-year-old was working long hours on his little holding. The unusual weather, for Bertrand du Gwezklen, orphan and poor hedge-squire, meant that more hours could be spent preparing the ground of the little bit of land his lord had given him in lieu of payment for his services as a soldier and bodyguard. It had always been Bertrand's dream to hold his own land, and this little scrap, which was not his by any stretch of the imagination, but which he could use, was the first step in that dream.

He was a short, nuggety little fellow with a plain, even ugly face: a squashed nose, bulging eyes, and an air of fierce determination that had made some nickname him *Kisaoz*, Bulldog. Like those fierce stubby dogs, he fought like a lion and already, at his age, had muscles like iron. For these skills he was already in high demand, and had been earning his own keep since he was eight years old, as a sword-carrier and squire and bodyguard to one of the lords of Broceliande. An orphan, whose parents had died long ago, he had little money, except for the little he'd been able to scrape together himself, and no education, for he had never been taught to read and write, or even any of the manners of a better-born squire who might aspire to become a courtly knight. And so he was well aware that his best hope for the future lay in being a very good mercenary soldier, perhaps even the leader of such a band. There were always various little fights and skirmishes amongst local lords, and foreign expeditions too, all kinds of possibilities for a brave and adventurous man.

Though Bertrand was unlearned, he was a long way from being a fool. He occupied the spare time he had in dreaming of a way that a truly efficient fighting force might be put together; his lord, in his cups, had spoken of the fact that one day, inevitably, there would be war with England, and thus plenty of scope for a man whose skills were all in battle, and whose heart was in the land.

The manor where Bertrand lived on the rare occasions when he was home was a large but not very productive one. Its lord, Sir Yann de Broceliande, was often away, and employed a steward who was either a crook, or incompetent, or both. Broceliande should have been one of the richest manors in that part of Brittany, but it was not. The story – perhaps put about by the crooked steward – was that, long ago, a Broceliande lord had offended an otherwordly lady, a fairy, and that she had put a curse on the manor and the family as a result. Bertrand was not at all sure he believed this. Of course, it was possible; the forest that gave the manor its name was a place of great enchantment, for it was the last resting-place of the great wizard Merlin, and its holy fountain attracted a stream of pilgrims and hopeful cripples. Fairies, the korrigans, undoubtedly inhabited its bright groves, and other spirits lurked in its shadowy places: but the story never said just who the lady had been, nor how long ago the curse had been put on the place. Bertrand had more than a suspicion that the manor's bad luck had happened rather more recently than 'a long time ago'. Say less than fifteen years ago. Say about as long as the tenure of the steward!

But Yann de Broceliande, on his infrequent visits back to the manor, would not hear a word spoken against his steward, despite the debts of the manor, despite the failed harvests and the thousand and one signs of something very wrong in the man's management. He was too trusting, perhaps. And too preoccupied with other things outside his manor. He was not a bad lord, by any means; indeed, he was kind. But he was distracted, unfocussed on his lands, and restless. Perhaps that was the curse put on him by the fairy. Or perhaps he was just like that. Who knew? Bertrand had no idea. He felt no oppression of the spirit in Broceliande himself, apart from one spot he avoided, like nearly all the local people: the clearing where a white oak stood, a place known as Dergwenn. That place had a strange reputation. But even the thought of Dergwenn did not change his feelings towards his home. Why should it? You just accepted what you could not change. And you did not tempt fate by wandering too close to areas known to be haunted.

Bertrand was always glad to get time off from fighting or bodyguarding so that he could scratch around in the soil. He was only there that late October because Yann de Broceliande's only daughter was getting married to a rich and powerful French baron, and the lord of Broceliande, in his joy – the Frenchman's moneybags might well help to revive Broceliande's flagging fortunes – had given Bertrand leave of absence for a few weeks. He had immediately returned to Brittany, and spent happy days with his friends on the manor, and with his beloved plants and small herd of goats.

This year he even had a pig, tethered in Broceliande Forest, getting fat on beechmast and acorns; usually, by this time, it would have been butchered, but he had allowed it to live a bit longer, to get a bit fatter, on account of the good weather. He would have sides of bacon, he thought, and air-cured ham, and fat meat to put in the soup, with winter greens! He thought often of food, did Bertrand, for he was often hungry. The food you got as a soldier on campaign or on tour was pretty miserable, unless you managed to steal some eggs or chickens or lamb from farms you passed through. And Bertrand, being a devoted farmer himself when he could, did not like doing that, for he knew how hard it was to raise livestock. He never joined in the looting which the others saw as part of the perks of soldiering. It did not do to antagonise people, he thought. Despite the laughter and muted jokes of the others (no-one was too mocking, though; they well knew Bertrand's fighting prowess) he much preferred parting with his hard-earned coins to pay for a few eggs or a bit of milk when he needed it. And when he didn't have any money, he went without those things. There were other ways to supplement your diet; traps that could be laid for wild things, like rabbits and hares and pigeons and so on. And Bertrand was very good at that. His surprisingly nimble fingers would work at a bit of stick, a length of thin rope or whippy reed, and delicately construct a deadly snare for some little wild beast or flying thing.

Truth to tell, Bertrand du Gwezklen was seen by many of his comrades as much as by his employer, as being a bit of a wild beast himself, with the virtues and vices of that kind. Loyal and devoted to a fault, never killing for pleasure but only because he had to, acting on instinct, shy yet direct, tough and brave yet modest, he could also be unpredictably hot-tempered, lacking in table or any other manners, rough and unkempt much of the time. But if he lacked civilised virtues, he also lacked civilised vices: there was no cruelty or treachery in him, though he possessed an instinctive, foxy cunning. And he had one thing which we are told by some of the saints that wild beasts, unlearned in churchy piety, nevertheless also know instinctively: a reverence for the sacred, a worship of their Creator, a love of God that is as inarticulate as it is deep. That was Bertrand; he never made a big deal of his prayers and other devotions, and indeed usually performed them hidden away from other people. Every year on Christmas Eve, if he was at Broceliande, he would visit one of the hermits who lived deep in the forest, bring modest gifts which he had collected during the year, and ask him to say prayers for the souls of all those people with no shelter in the world.

Bertrand was deeply grateful for his own shelter and place in the world, and knew that it was not given to all, especially to a poor orphan, to be so fortunate. Yann de Broceliande might be many things, not many of them very nice, but he was a Breton and thus had the knowledge of his ancient obligations as a clan leader. Bertrand's parents had been loyal retainers, and distant relatives of his, as were most of the other people on the manor, and he would no more have thought of turning Bertrand out when they died than of cutting off his own finger. It was not always the way of the world beyond Brittany, Bertrand knew; the plague had thrown many things into chaos, including the old system which even if it meant lords had a great deal of power over people on their manor, also meant they were obliged to look after them. Many of the French and English and Burgundian and Norman soldiers Bertrand had fought with had been thrown off land where their forebears had always lived, or had their villages destroyed by marauders, and nowhere to live, no way to live either, if it had not been for soldiering. Beggars were very numerous now in all the cities, and everyone's hearts seemed to have hardened against them. Charity was not a popular virtue, in the hard-scrabble fourteenth century. Faith – well, that had also gone by the board, for many people. And hope . . . well, there were many who said these were the last days of the world.

Bertrand rarely worried about that. He rarely thought beyond his small dreams of holding a bit of land, doing his duty honestly and well as a soldier, and perhaps one day being the leader of a band of fighting men, hiring out their services. But as to having a family or rising in the world, well, he never even *dreamed* it. He knew he was too ugly, too poor, too unlearned, to attract any self-respecting girl; and the ones who *didn't* respect themselves, he wanted nothing to do with! No, he thought, he would live and die a bachelor, and be content. He could retire, after a long period in the armies, and raise pigs and lambs on his bit of ground, and join in the thousand and one tasks of a manor.

As to rising in the world – he had seen a fair bit of the world, outside Broceliande; and he had no interest in rising there. Folks were pretty much the same outside as in, he knew; passions ran the same ways in Court as much as in the fields, but the difference was that many at Court hid their game. Bertrand had seen a great deal of ugly things in his short life, and he had few illusions on the goodness of people. But he never dwelt on it. Everyone could be good, he had decided; many, maybe most people, maybe all people at one time or the other, except for the Blessed Virgin and Our Lord, had chosen not to be. People were not angels, nor devils, but something in between, and it was pointless seeing it otherwise. Bertrand certainly did not worry his head about it, but accepted people as they were, and kept his counsel. And though he did not know it, these unusual qualities of his were observed, and commented upon, and approved, and the knowledge filed away for future reference.

Three

On that bright October morning, Dame Viviane was setting off, rather reluctantly, on an unexpected journey. Her sister Nolwenn, who still lived near the Forest of Broceliande, where she had been born, had been taken very ill. Indeed, said the letter from Nolwenn's neighbour, which Viviane had received a couple of days before, she was close to death, and had been asking for Viviane constantly. The letter was dated a few days previously; it was written not in the neighbour's script, for the good Widow Kemener could not read or write, but in a clerk's curling handwriting. That alone was enough to convince Viviane that this was serious news; Widow Kemener, let alone Nolwenn, would never have paid over the goodly amount of silver required to pay a clerk to write the letter, if things were not bad. Viviane did not like leaving Raguenel at this time of the year; but there was no help for it. At least the weather was good, and she should be able to accomplish the whole trip in under a week, and hopefully get back to the manor before Hallowe'en.

She had spoken at great and rather severe length to the children, instructing them on what they were and were not to do. Tiphaine had listened with a bright and attentive face; but Gromer wore a sulky expression. It annoyed Viviane, and troubled her a little, and so she had played it safe by appointing her three closest familiars, Estik, the nightingale, Lenaik, the wren, and Penduik, the song-thrush, to watch over them. She had also, without telling the children or indeed the three birds, contrived two extra precautions: she had asked old Hopernoz, the screech owl, to keep an eye on them at night, for Estik, Lenaik and Penduik were day-birds. And she had also made a warding talisman to protect the children from real danger. This came in the form of a little willow-and-thorn knot, sewn into the bottom of the little purses the children wore at their waists. Into the knots had been woven the echoes of several powerful words, and the whole had been bound with Viviane's own treaty with Rouanez, the Queen of the local korrigans. Only Rouanez had anything like the power needed to break the spell, and she would not do it. Viviane and she had a long-standing understanding, which would not be willingly broken on either side.

Now, however, just as she was about to set off, doubts gnawed at her again. She would never have told the children – it was not her place to do so – but she loved them dearly, as if they were the children she had never had herself. Her choice as a young woman had been to forgo all that side of life, in order to concentrate on the task of continuing to maintain the old ways, the old methods of protection against the disruption of the world by the forces of mischief and chaos. As the seventh daughter of a seventh daughter, who had very early on shown signs of the Sight, Viviane had been marked out from the beginning as one of those rare talented human creatures who might deal equally with otherworlders. Depending on the quality and range of their talent, such Sighted people were allowed to reach a level of contact with the Otherworld that others could only hope for – or fear.

Viviane herself had long ago reached understanding not only with the local korrigans, but many others from that Otherworld the humans called Faerie. Indeed, she had been accepted as a Guardian – one of those humans who keep the ways of otherworlders and humans both separate, yet intermingled. Guardians – who were never appointed, for Faerie was not a world of appointments and officialdom – had, in the offhand, yet fateful, manner of such things, to make their own way, and express their protective talents differently. Viviane's way was not that of old Merlin, with his books, and his knowledge of the future; hers was the more humble, yet perhaps more difficult, way, of the living natural world. And so she understood the tongues of animals, too, and could even make out some of the silent speech of plants. But her speciality was birds; in particular the little song-birds of field and hedgerow. They were her confidants and spies, though many of them could be silly and empty-headed. Estik, Lenaik and Penduik were the cleverest, the most loyal and brave, and she was sacrificing something of her own safety by leaving them with Tiphaine and Gromer. She was also taking a gamble asking old Hopernoz to help – the owls were the most unpredictable of the birds. But Hopernoz's territory encompassed Raguenel.

He could be trusted to be loyal to that, at least. And so it had to be done.

Viviane's experiences had made her deep and rich in knowledge and power; but though, as a Guardian, she could have had access permanently to the ease and luxury of Faerie, she had chosen to remain in the world of her fellow humans, appearing as a scatty and sometimes fierce old lady, the better to protect and disarm. She had become the *genius loci*, the spirit of place, the guardian angel, of Raguenel, for every place needed one such. And it had brought her happiness, of a kind. Happiness that was to end, soon; for the children would leave Raguenel, and her work here would be done. She would have to move on to another place, other children, who might need her special services.

At the beginning, when she was young, she had accepted her own calling as Guardian with some difficulty. Indeed, she had fought against it. Such was often the way with the genuinely talented, for those who tried to force on such talents, or tried to force the Otherworld to bend to their will, like sorcerers, acted quite differently. It was not power the Guardians sought, but balance, and trust: and as with many other things, those who grasped at their task too eagerly could be corrupted more easily.

Over time, Viviane had become resigned, even accepting, of her fate. But even now, occasionally, she regretted it. She would sometimes wish she had been like her siblings, who had grown up as ordinary people in a world that for them was solid and time-defined, not full of timeless shadows and half-things that must be kept in balance if the world was to survive. However, mostly, she was happy enough with her lot, for it had given her much.

But Nolwenn was the last of her siblings left alive. For along with her special powers, Viviane had been given a gift – or was it a curse? It was a long, long life. Nolwenn was the youngest in the family, for twelve children had been born, in all, to Viviane's and Nolwenn's parents, and all of them, remarkably, had survived into adulthood. There had been many children born to *those* children, as well. But Viviane and Nolwenn were the only ones left of that generation. And Nolwenn was reckoned to be a very old lady, in the village where she lived. But Viviane was still fit and heartily healthy, her heart pumping as strong and steadily as it had always done, her limbs limber, her mind active. Some people said she was over one hundred years old. Others that she was closer to ninety. Viviane told no-one what the truth was. And in truth, she had forgotten. Age meant very little to her.

For quite a long time now – since Tiphaine and Gromer's births, perhaps – Viviane had felt a sense of calm and happiness suffusing the little world in which she lived. Nothing had threatened the twins in all the long years she had cared for them. Nothing, either from the tumultuous human march of history outside, or from the mischievous or whimsical or more dangerous realms, had attempted to break the web of enchantment and peace that Viviane's mind had succeeded in spinning around the manor. Though people within it did not always recognise it, Raguenel was a little bright spot, a remote little Eden, a place almost out of time. That had been Viviane's mission: to arm and protect the Raguenel children not by teaching them too much magic, but by surrounding them with joy and love and beauty until they grew old enough, and were confident enough, to understand that all was not that way in any of the worlds.

She did not regret that choice. They had grown to be beautiful, light-filled, happy children whose very presence would be enough to bless any place where they might be, later. From the first time she had come across Raguenel, the first time she had laid eyes on the babies, Viviane had known this place, these people, were very important, not just to themselves, but to very many more, to strangers as well as family. These children would hold the fate of many in their hands, she had seen that straight away; and though she did not know exactly what sort of part they would play on the great stage of human affairs, she knew she was needed here, to help to prepare them, in spirit and heart.

Even now, when a tiny unease had begun to twine its way into her mind, Viviane did not think that the children would be in danger. She had carefully scouted the atmosphere of Raguenel, and found it unchanged from how it usually was. She had sent Estik, Lenaik and Penduick on reconnaissance missions amongst the birds and animals, and they had reported calm, too. There was no sense of anything waiting, anything of a malevolent presence. The korrigans, yes; they were always close. But they were never evil. Only whimsical, unpredictable, and annoying sometimes. But with a great sense of honour, even in their mischief. Rouanez, their queen, might not be altogether a comfortable character, but she kept well to her people's code. The others – the *duzigs*, or dwarfs, the mary-morgans, or water spirits, and the myriad of swarming races that inhabited the underworld of Faerie – they were not malicious, generally, either. As long as the children kept to the rule of not going to Stone Wood on those two days of the year, the denizens of Faerie regarded them, if not benevolently, at least with the shallow, sparkling indifference of their kind.

Viviane was old and deep enough to know that despite all these things, there could still be problems. Things could change in an instant. Secret darkness might be hidden too far for her to see. Accidents could happen. Hence her unease, hence the warding charms. But all things considered, on balance, it was fairly safe. She could not just ignore Nolwenn's plight.

Though she and Nolwenn had never been particularly close – Viviane's favourite sister had been long-dead Fanchon – she was the last of her siblings. That counted for something, in all worlds. If Viviane did not go to see Nolwenn, she would always regret it. And, in some strange way, she was convinced that if she did not go, it would also spell disaster for Raguenel, for these children she loved, and for a great many people beyond, who were not even aware yet of their existence.

No, she must go. They had the birds, and the hidden charms; and she had also instructed several people to keep a close eye on the twins' comings and goings.

When at last, after many kisses, hugs, and last-minute repetitions of instructions, she set off on her sturdy little pony for the long ride through the forests, she was feeling as relaxed as she could be, under the circumstances. Her last sight of the children, as she

26

rounded the bend which would lead her across the ford and into Stone Wood, was of a bright-eyed Tiphaine, waving madly, and a Gromer attempting to be manly and restrained, but with a kind of leashed eagerness to him.

Once again, the little spasm of unease gripped at her; and she said an extra charm, just for Gromer. She sent it flying quietly to sit on his shoulder like a tiny invisible sparrow, there to whisper useful and safe pastimes into his ear, and his mind. It seemed a pity, to so restrict his energies; but it was necessary. It would keep him, and his sister, safe. For it was Gromer who was most at risk, she'd known that from a long time back. Most at risk, because the risk came from his own nature.

Tiphaine, now, that was a different story. She could be trusted much more instinctively.

Muttering to herself, she turned her pony's head in the direction of Broceliande. She must press on, for there was much to do.

Four

The forest of Broceliande, on a sunny holiday, was popular with everybody. Bertrand wasn't the only person abroad at an early hour that day. He said good morning to at least five people in the space of as few minutes; someone herding a pig, like him, someone picking up sticks for the fire, a couple of young lovers cooing and kissing under a tree, an old man gathering late mushrooms. A little further on, he met one of the forest's hermits, Sieur Gwazig, who was kneeling, tending an injured magpie by the side of the path. He looked up as he heard Bertrand's approach, and his face cleared. 'Ah . . . it's you. Come here. Need your help.'

Sieur Gwazig was a man of few words, and those mostly abrupt, but he had an infinite gentleness of nature. He was not a priest or a monk, but a man who lived as a hermit in the forest, for what reason, whether secret sorrow or dangerous past, no-one knew, or asked about. He was one of the few people who was not afraid of the great white oak, Dergwenn, and in his case it seemed neither foolhardy nor ignorant, but genuinely fearless. It was as if he had already seen everything that could possibly frighten him, and had surmounted each and every one of those fears, so that a white oak in a magic-haunted clearing was not nothing to him, but no more than any other thing. It was one of the unusual things about him, but not the most unusual, by a long way.

Now, Bertrand did as he was asked. He held the panic-stricken bird gently but firmly as Sieur Gwazig felt it all over, clucking to himself, while the bird's yellow eyes glared in pain and fear. Then the hermit's surprisingly long and delicate fingers moved like lightning over the bird's injured wing as he sang a few words under his breath, and Bertrand saw quite clearly how the bends in the bird's limb moved under his fingers, straightening like a bent metal rod can be reshaped in the forge. He knew about the hermit's extraordinary healing, or rather, bone-knitting, powers – some called Sieur Gwazig, under their breath, Bonemender – but it still took his breath away, every time. It was miraculous, no question. And nobody did question it, least of all Gwazig himself. His fame had spread beyond Broceliande now, and in the summer, numerous crippled and hopeful pilgrims came to see him at his home in the cave near the spring. But despite this, he had stayed the same shy, abrupt, gentle, limping, sad-eyed, thin, stooping man who had suddenly appeared in Broceliande one evening many, many years ago. Nobody knew where he had come from, or what his real name was, or how old he was, though, given human ingenuity and curiosity, there were a dozen rumours to explain all these things. Some said he was an aristocrat, even a prince, who had fallen on hard times, or been through an injustice; others said he was a criminal who had reformed; or a recovered madman; others that he was a secret sorcerer. Bertrand spared little thought for such speculations. He liked Gwazig, and admired him, and, occasionally, was disturbed by that gift of his – though not so much by the other, his beautiful singing voice, and love of music. For him, anyway, it was by their fruits that you knew a man or woman, and Gwazig's fruits were very sweet indeed.

The hermit stroked the bird's wings. He touched the bird's head, slightly. 'Let it go, now.'

Bertrand opened his hand, and released the bird. Gwazig shook his head. 'It hurt your hand.'

'S nothing,' said Bertrand, sucking at the thumb the bird had pecked in its panic. He watched as the magpie tottered a step or two, its beak opening and closing as if in astonishment; smiled as the wing that had been injured lifted gently, then more vigorously, with the good one. The bird took a few more steps, then launched itself and rose into the air, both wings going together. Bertrand and Gwazig watched it out of sight.

'Wouldn't mind being able to do that,' said Bertrand, at last.

'Flying? It's not all you might think.' Gwazig spoke absently, but Bertrand, surprised, saw the hermit's grey eyes were shining with something close to savage regret. A little shiver rippled over him as he remembered the villagers' stories. Then the hermit saw his expression, and smiled. 'I imagine,' he went on, smoothly. 'I've dreamt of it. And have you never dreamt of flying, Bertrand? Have you not felt the surge at your chest, in your dreams?'

'Well . . . I have, but that's dreams. Can't be done, by a man, in real life.'

The hermit nodded. 'You are right.' He frowned. 'Bertrand, how early were you up this morning?'

'Early enough,' said Bertrand, a little questioningly. Gwazig rose slowly to his feet. 'Did you happen to see an owl, this morning? A big owl? Very much bigger than any we've ever seen in these parts?'

Bertrand stared. 'No.'

'I saw . . . this morning . . . one coming from the direction of Dergwenn. Never seen such a big one.' Gwazig's expression was curiously intense.

Bertrand shook his head. 'No, Sieur Gwazig, I saw no owl.' Unease hammered at him as he looked into the hermit's eyes, and saw . . . what? Fear? Excitement? A barely leashed-in savagery? He was not sure, and not sure he wanted to know, either.

Gwazig frowned a little. 'Well, I —' He broke off as a woman came running down the path towards them, holding up something in her hand. It was Widow Kemener. 'Sieur Gwazig! Sieur Gwazig!' she called as she ran. 'A letter's come for you! It is important!'

'A letter,' echoed Gwazig, in a low voice. Bertrand was astonished to see the colour had drained out of his face. But before he could say anything, Widow Kemener had reached them, and thrust the letter at the hermit. Bertrand only had time to glimpse an official-looking red wax seal, imprinted with . . . some kind of figurehead? He had no time for anything more than a glimpse, though, because Gwazig swiftly put the letter away in his clothes, nodded at the woman and Bertrand, and set off briskly down the path, without another word.

'Well, then!' said Widow Kemener, shrugging. 'He's in a hurry, right enough, but I reckons I knows what 'tis . . . a summons, from the Duke and Duchess theirselves!'

'How do you know that?' said Bertrand, looking, though he didn't know it, rather fierce himself.

'Stands to reason, boy,' said the woman, comfortably. ' 'Tis important – has a wax seal on it with an image of the Duke – bound to be! Ah, yes, I always knew he was a dark horse, that one,' she went on, nodding with satisfaction, and Bertrand knew the story of Sieur Gwazig's summons by the Duke would be common knowledge by nightfall. He was not interested in silly speculation, though. It was none of any of their business.

He said a rather curt goodbye to Widow Kemener, and set off again after his pig, which had taken off after some scent of its own. He thought a little of the letter Sieur Gwazig had received, and then of the strange thing he'd said, about the big owl coming from Dergwenn, and then forgot both in the simple and satisfying pleasures of a whole day left alone to roam at his leisure in the forest of Broceliande.

Five

A day passed, then two, then three. The weather
stayed fresh and fair at Raguenel, and the
children stayed happy. They fished and swam and ran
riot with the other village children, and the little manor
had never seemed so beautiful to them. Sometimes,
Tiphaine thought that this would go on forever; that
she and Gromer would never have to grow up, that
somehow Dame Viviane had contrived to put a stop to
the dull passage of time. They missed her, a little;
but only a little. There was so much to do, so many
playmates of their own age, that even the kindest, wisest
adult was nothing more than part of the furniture, not
to be missed with any ache when they were away. And
the birds, Estik, Lenaik and Penduik were merry little
companions too, taking their duties seriously enough,
but in the nature of their kind, darting and quick and
cheerful, so that the children hardly felt like they were
being watched over at all.

But the little unease Viviane had felt when she looked
at Gromer was not without cause. In that strange,
enchanted autumn, the boy had started to feel the

stirrings of something he could not understand; something that tugged at the corners of his mind, like a little thread, tweaking. He could not put a name to this feeling, still less words of any kind; and so he had not said anything to anyone about it, not even to Tiphaine, sister of his heart, best friend of his soul. He did not need to, in any case; the twins shared heartstrings. And if his own talent was rapidly showing itself to be an extraordinary deftness of hand and eye, Tiphaine's was slowly crystallising as a preternatural sensitivity to tiny clues in the mind. Tiphaine had been aware for quite a while of the unease at the edge of Gromer's mind, but like him, she did not know how to explain what she saw. Her talent was still young and unpractised; and this feeling was so formless, so light and elusive, more like a piece of spider's silk wafting in the breeze after a web has been broken, than a real thread, a tight thing. It was to do with the end of things here, she knew that, in an unspoken way. She had a sadness on her about that too, though like Gromer, she had no desire to disobey her parents' wishes. But Gromer's unease was different to hers, too. She had thought that was perhaps because she was a girl, and he a boy, and now at this moment in their lives, they would no longer be Tiphaine-and-Gromer, flesh of one flesh, almost one being, but diverging, Tiphaine and Gromer, one to be a lady, the other a knight. One to learn woman's ways; the other to enter a man's world. It was inevitable. In some ways, it even excited her. But in others, if she thought about it, she felt afraid.

But at least in those days whilst Viviane was away, Gromer seemed cheerful. It was almost as if the little unease had finally blown away in the wind. His mind, when Tiphaine groped for it, was unruffled. And she herself felt at peace, happy, in a way that she knew she would always remember, no matter what happened to them in their lives afterwards.

Estik, Lenaik and Penduik had taken to meeting in the stables every dusk, just after the children had gone into the manor-house to have their supper. It was a time when they knew they could relax their watchfulness; though Viviane had not told them of Hopernoz's role, they knew, intuitively, that she would have had to do something about protecting the twins' night, too. The little birds hated and feared the owls, and kept well out of Hopernoz's way, or indeed any of the owls, of whatever kind they were. But they had sensed his passage, heard his low whistle as he emerged for his night hunting, and felt the way the night was rippled, ever so softly, by his silent wings as he circled the manor every night. They knew that he, too, was part of a strange alliance centred on Viviane's protection of Raguenel. And so, though they never mentioned him, or any other owl – the very name *Toud*, the clan name of all owls in Brittany, was hedged about with taboos amongst the little birds – they could sleep a little better, in their warm hiding-places, knowing the hunter of the night was also watching for intruders.

One particular dusk, just a day or so away from the dangerous period of Hallowe'en and the days after – which amongst the birds was known as Shadow Time – Estik, Lenaik and Penduik met as usual in the stables, in a disused manger that was full of bits of grass seed. Lenaik had something to report, something she was bursting with, that agitated wildly in her little head.

'Something's happening in korrigan-country,' she said, hopping about in her nervy, perky way. She pecked at a grass seed. 'I met Lapous today in the meadow, and he told me that he saw something quite strange, just yesterday.'

Lapous was a skylark, and a notorious, inveterate gossip, pouring out streams of rumour and innuendo at the top of his voice. Penduik ruffled her feathers and said, sharply, 'You shouldn't be listening to that emptyhead.'

'No, but you see, this is different. He saw Rouanez out in broad daylight! Just yesterday!'

The other two stared at her, momentarily still. Then Estik said, slowly, 'But it's not Shadow Time, yet . . .'

'No. So why should the Queen of the Korrigans be moving in broad daylight? It's dangerous for her.'

'And for everyone else,' said Penduik, grimly.

'If Lapous is telling the truth . . .' Estik cocked her head to one side. 'Can we ever believe him?'

'He was scared,' said Lenaik. 'I've never seen him like that.'

'He could have imagined it.' Penduik was trying to make the best of it.

'He could have. Heaven knows he does it often enough. But he wasn't singing about this, my friends. He was huddled in a corner of the meadow, worrying about it. If I hadn't come across him, I doubt he would have told anyone. But he had to tell someone, you know what I mean?'

The other two bobbed their heads. Yes, they knew – and they knew, too, that if a songbird – and especially one like a skylark whose very essence was song – did not make a song out of every bit of news and experience that came along, then something was very wrong.

'He was happy to tell me,' said Lenaik. 'He looked very much better when I left him.'

'Of course,' snapped Penduik. 'Now you're in danger too. It spreads the load, for Lapous.'

'Oh, don't you see!' Lenaik hopped with impatience. 'Something must be happening, with the korrigans, if Rouanez is out during the day, clear to be seen, before the right time! Lapous said she was clear as clear, not at all shadowy or elusive. He saw her in a field near Stone Wood, on the opposite side from here. She was heading to the south. She was dressed like a peasant girl, but her ebony hair and her green eyes were unmistakeable, he said. Every bird within miles would know her for what she was. She had not troubled to disguise herself well. And yet she was moving stealthily, rapidly, urgently.'

'Worse and worse,' said Estik. 'If Rouanez gets to hear we saw her, or anyone did—'

Lenaik's whole body spasmed. She said, faintly, 'I know. But don't you see? It could be what Viviane was afraid of. She said to watch out for anything unusual. And this is very unusual.'

Penduik said, 'But it has nothing to do with Raguenel. You said Lapous saw her on the other side of Stone Wood, heading south. In the *opposite* direction to here. The korrigans have never interfered with us. Or with Raguenel.'

'They may not now,' said Lenaik. 'And, just as you say, it may have nothing to do with us, just korrigan business of one sort or the other. But perhaps we should find out why Rouanez was abroad, and where she was going.'

There was silence, broken after a short while by Estik.

'Very well. But what do you propose, Lenaik?'

'We have to let Viviane know immediately. One of us must find her,' she said, promptly, as if she'd been thinking of little else, which indeed was the truth. 'We have to protect the children, and prevent them from going anywhere near Stone Wood, come what may. One of us must stay and do that. And one of us must try and find out what is going on. I've already found out everything from Lapous, he cannot tell us any more.' She broke off, suddenly. Her throat trembled. 'And that means the night. It means . . . it means either we brave the night ourselves; or we . . . we go to see Hopernoz, and ask him to watch for us.'

Estik and Penduik were silent. Ripples of unease moved at their throats, too. Lenaik went on, hesitantly, 'I . . . perhaps you, Penduik, should go to find Viviane . . . you, Estik, should stay here with the children, and I . . .' She broke off. The other two birds did not look at her, but pecked absently at the grass seeds. Broceliande was a fair distance, tiringly so for any non-migratory bird; but it was feasible. Looking after two lively and unpredictable human children was work enough for three birds, let alone one; but it was feasible. Going into the night – braving its terrors and its hunger, and coming face to face with the riders of night themselves, silent death on the wing – that was the ultimate fear for little birds, the ultimate foolishness, an act without precedent, as far as those three knew. Lenaik was going into unknown territory, if she did it.

And neither Estik nor Penduik was able to offer any help, one way or the other.

Lenaik knew it, too. She could simply have gone back on what she had said. No-one would have blamed her. She was a wren. Oh, not an ordinary wren; for what creature could stay ordinary, when once they had taken part in the half-world of the Guardians? Being Viviane's familiar had irrevocably changed her, set her aside from the common run of wrens, as Estik had been set apart from the common run of nightingales, and Penduik from the common run of thrushes. But she was, still, a wren. And for a wren, owls were Enemy, just as for an owl, wrens were Prey. Her wrenness, Hopernoz's owlness – would their contact with Viviane be enough to overcome that, if only for a moment? Perhaps. Perhaps not. She did not know. She had no way of knowing.

'I will go to see Hopernoz,' she said, firmly, and swallowed a particularly juicy grass seed, as if she had no care at all. 'I know where he lives. If I go at dawn, he will be already replete, and he will be tired. There will be no danger. You'll see.'

'Yes,' said Penduick, very low and troubled. Estik said nothing, but flew to another manger, and, under the startled eyes of its occupant, pecked wildly about. By this, Lenaik knew that the nightingale was almost beside himself with superstitious fear. A fear that gripped at her own little body. But it was too late now to go back on her words.

Meanwhile, Tiphaine and Gromer were getting ready for bed. They were tired. It had been a long, happy, active day. Later, they would remember it, separately and together, as a kind of antechamber day. A sort of sunny passageway before a door opened: a dark and secret door. Like the reversal of what usually happened, when you went from darkness, through a door, into light.

But that evening, they had no such thoughts. They squabbled companionably for a moment or two over who was going to have the great illustrated manuscript of fables to look at that night, and decided, as they always did, that they would look at it together, and read the fables to each other, as they had done ever since they could read, which was not very long ago. The manuscript had been made by a visiting clerk, a distant cousin of the Viscount's, who had presented the family with it as a thanks for his long stay. The children had not liked the man – he was impatient and abrupt and did not like children hanging over him while he created the delicate pictures and wrote the fables in his flowing hand – but they loved his book. They knew the stories off by heart, but it did not matter. And the pictures were so real to them, somehow; the foxes and wolves and crows and bears and other animals and birds looked like they might step out from the margins, which enclosed them like magic barriers. You could see animals just like them in the woods and the fields and the meadows; and the people who sometimes appeared with them had faces you might see in any village or down any path. This was the natural world, the world of sunlight and shadow. But curling and lacing in the initial letters were other creatures, too, creatures from other worlds, half-disguised, gazing out slyly, or startled, or impassively from the gold and red and black of the artist's line.

'Let's read the story of the Lion and the Fox,' said Tiphaine, as they gently turned the pages, trying to decide.

'No,' said Gromer, more for the principle of it than because he really disagreed. 'I want to read the Hare and the Tortoise.'

'We read that the other night,' said Tiphaine.

'So?' There was an imp of mischief in Gromer tonight.

'So we can't. We should read something different.'

'Who says?'

'I do.'

'And who are you? Just silly Gromer. It's my turn to choose.'

'No, it's mine.'

She was trying to turn the page, and so was he. The manuscript crackled in their hands. Tiphaine snapped:

'Careful! You'll tear it!'

'You will.'

'Oh, stop it.'

'You do.' Gromer had managed to turn a page. And it was not on either of those fables, but another on which he fell. They looked at each other. This was one they both liked.

Tiphaine smiled. 'Shall we?'

'Why not?' shrugged Gromer.

Tiphaine touched the page. She said, running her finger under the words, 'The Wolf, the Bull, and the Ermine.' She and Gromer looked at the picture. It was one of their favourites, for it was full of action. There was a picture of a big grey wolf fighting with a huge black bull, in an oak forest, by the side of a pit, and in the pit, only just seen, eyes aglow, a little white ermine. There was blood on the wolf's flanks, where he'd been gored by the bull, and a ragged wound on the side of the bull, where he'd been savaged by the wolf's sharp teeth. But the ermine was clean and white and whole, its body gleaming against the darkness of the pit. And around the pit, in shadow, and clustered near the ermine, were all sorts of strange creatures, half seen.

'Read it,' said Gromer.

Tiphaine began, 'In the oakwood, the wolf waited for the bull. And the bull knew the wolf was there, and walked carefully. But in the pit in the wood, the ermine waited for them both. The wolf and the bull met each other, unexpectedly, and the wolf gave a howl, and the bull gave a bellow, and they charged each other. But the ermine in the pit called out, so only the bull could hear, Sir Bull, you should win! Gore him in the stomach! And I will help you! And so the bull charged, and caught the wolf on the side of his body. Then the ermine called out, so only the wolf could hear, Oh, Sir Wolf, poor Sir Wolf, you must show him who's master, and tear at him with your teeth, and your claws! For I am on your side! And so the wolf ran at the bull, and caught him unexpectedly on one side, so that his warm blood flowed. And the ermine nosed her way a little out of the pit, and she said, yes, that's right, fight each other, only one can win! And I am on your side! Maddened by blood and by pain and by fear, the wolf and bull kept charging each other, and wounding each other, so grievously till at last they inflicted a fatal blow. And when each of them lay dying, the ermine climbed out of the pit, and she stood regarding them both, and she said, Oh, Sir Wolf, and Sir Bull, a sad day it was for you both that you came to this oakwood. For it is my wood, and you are dying. And I have won.'

'I like that story,' said Gromer.

'I don't really understand it,' said Tiphaine.

'No, neither do I – but it is a good story.'

They sat looking at the page for a little while longer, then Tiphaine yawned, and said, 'I'm tired.'

'I'm not,' said Gromer. But he was, really; and he proved it by yawning a yawn that nearly split his head in two, and made his sister laugh at him. So, still squabbling companionably, they went to bed, leaving the book lying open on top of the chest, instead of putting it away, as they usually did. And there it stayed, quietly, in the dark of the night, and the moonlight, until, in the very depths of the night hours, something swift and silent fluttered on to the pages, like a moth, then settled deeper into the book, which received it with a kind of shiver.

Six

$\mathcal{N}$ one of the three little birds could rest that
night. Each was filled with a nameless fear, a
sense of a storm, something approaching inexorably,
but whose shape or kind they could not guess. Lenaik,
of course, had the closest, most sharp fear; but neither
of the other two were at all at peace.

When the night was at its darkest, just before dawn,
they farewelled each other. Penduik prepared to begin
the long journey to Broceliande; Lenaik to confront
Hopernoz at his hollow tree; Estik to look after the
children as best he could. They did not speak of fears
any more, just of work that must be done. Each was
more alone than they had ever been, each carrying
within them the secret terror that they could indeed do
nothing, that they would let Viviane down completely.

Lenaik left first. Her companions farewelled her with
little cries and taps of the beak, the solemn leavetaking
of little birds who do not know if they will be alive at
the end of the day. She responded in kind, trying not to
listen too much to the wild flutterings of her over-

extended heart. She had the password Viviane had given them all; she would call it before she got to Hopernoz' tree. He would not hurt her. She was sure of it. He would not. She gave a little defiant twirl of her wings as she left, flying into the dark sky even now lighting up with the gold and pink splashes of dawn.

She flew on towards the big hollow tree at the edge of the wood where she knew Hopernoz roosted during the day, well-camouflaged against the bark. Her eyes peered desperately into the lightening air, for she was determined to catch sight of him before he, with his usually sharp senses lulled by approaching day, should see her. Ah. There was the tree. There was the hole where . . . her heart gave a great leap. She could see a pair of huge eyes – the round yellow-and-black eyes of an owl – blinking sleepily there in the opening, and an impression of a body huddled beyond, shifting into daytime immobility. Lenaik could not help it: she closed her eyes, for the glare, however softened by weariness, of owl-eyes, was so terrifying that she could not keep her wits about her. Of course, she then plunged to earth, falling stunned at the very foot of Hopernoz's tree.

It was a soft landing. She had fallen on to something soft . . . something . . . There was a smell . . .

Her eyes flew open. She was lying on feathers. Feathers! No, not just feathers. A body. A feathered body. The body of . . . of an *owl*. As her fuddled brain took hold of this amazing fact, another hit her almost as hard. The eyes in the tree. The yellow owl eyes, the huddled body in the tree. They were not those of Hopernoz, for he lay dead beneath her, on the ground. In the next moment, there was a whoosh of air, an agonising pain, and there were those terrible eyes, glaring down at her, no longer sleepy, but wide awake, and a huge form bent over her, her body held down by enormously powerful talons. This owl was much, much bigger than Hopernoz. She had never seen, or imagined, even in her worst nightmares, anything like it. Her poor over-extended heart gave way in that instant, and she fell into darkness and shadows.

Penduik left less than an hour after Lenaik had gone. She flapped on into the dawn air without incident, and covered quite a distance as the sun rose higher and higher into the sky. She met quite a number of other travellers in the wilderness of the heavens, and spent a little time greeting them. The further she got from Raguenel, strangely, the more her spirits lifted. She began to feel that Lenaik was exaggerating the dangers. After all, all that Lapous had seen had been Rouanez travelling far from home. It was not usual for korrigans to do so; they were homing spirits, but then, they were whimsical too. You never knew what they might take it into their heads to do.

Midday came, and she was still some way from Broceliande. She was tired, and the urgency of her mission had altogether left her. She landed in a meadow at the edge of a wood, and found a nice sunny hidden spot in which to rest, and some tasty food to eat. She was preening herself when she suddenly heard a low call; a call that made all her body bristle with delight. It was the call of another song-thrush; but one she had never heard before, with a yearning edge to it that seemed to speak directly to her heart. She could not help herself. She answered, softly. Silence, then the call came again, and this time, the note was so thrilling that Penduik called, 'Who are you? Oh, show yourself to me,' while her heart fluttered in sheer joy. She had quite forgotten her task, the korrigans, Raguenel, the children, Viviane, her companions, everything but the sweetness of the voice calling her.

The other thrush whispered, echoing her softly, 'Who are you? Who are you?'

'I am Penduik ... I am Penduik ... Oh, show yourself to me ...'

'Here I am,' said the other thrush, and there, indeed, he was, landing beside her. She had never seen such a beautiful bird. His eyes were bright, his feathers touched with glimmer. In that instant, Penduik's overexcited heart gave way completely, and she fell into the sweet, sunny forgetfulness of love, and all thoughts or remembrance of her original home fled from her flighty little mind, not to return till it was far too late.

The children were awake early, and in fine and lively spirits. Poor Estik, exhausted by his sleepless night, had a hard time keeping track of them as they rampaged through the manor-house, into the gardens and into the meadows beyond. It was another beautiful day, still a day away from Shadow Time. There was a golden stillness to the air that was most soothing, but also most soporific for any tired creature. Estik tried valiantly to do the job he had been left to do, but he could not help snatching a few minutes' nap every so often, only to reopen his eyes with a start, a few minutes later. But Gromer and Tiphaine were still safely there, playing, jumping, skipping, all the many things children did. In the normal run of things, Estik would have been happy to join in, but today it merely made him feel even more tired.

At last, by early afternoon, even the children were tired. They undressed to their underclothes and settled down in their sunswept room, mumbling sleepily to each other over the book of fables. Estik sat on a sunny, sheltered bit of the windowseat, well hidden by a fold of curtain, and watched them benevolently. They were safe. They would be safe. It was not yet Shadow Time. Tomorrow was the day to worry about. Today, they were safe . . . safe . . . his eyes began to close . . . to open . . . to close . . . to open . . . to close . . . to . . . stay closed. His head dropped under his wing. He was asleep. And soon, fast asleep.

The children read on for a little while more, but they too began to nod over the book. Sunlight washed gently over them as they put their own heads under their arms, and fell asleep, softly, quietly, in the pleasant air. Scattered on the floor beside their beds were their clothes, including their belts with the little purses on them, containing the warding talismans Viviane had so painstakingly constructed.

A voice was calling Gromer. 'Gromer . . . Gromer, great knight, champion of the world!'

Gromer followed the direction of the voice. And saw, in the window, framed in the opening, the biggest owl he had ever seen. It was the size of a small child. Its eyes were huge, yellow, very bright but not cold, as most birds' eyes are, but full of a warm, humorous, almost human intelligence. The owl's beak was like that of an eagle, its massive body well-covered with soft, thick, tawny and creamy feathers. It had heavily feathered toes, and feathered protuberances like quiffs of hair to either side of its eyes.

Gromer stared at the owl for a moment; then he said, rubbing at his eyes, 'Excuse me, but was it you who spoke to me?'

The owl regarded Gromer with great good humour, and said, 'Of course.'

'Am I dreaming?' said Gromer.

'Perhaps,' said the owl. 'And if you're dreaming, what would happen in your dream, next?' It moved slightly, so Gromer could see the way the great body rippled, but its eyes stayed on Gromer, who felt as though he were being drawn towards the great bird.

'I would fly over the whole world, and see everything, and be the master of it all,' he said.

The owl said, 'My back is wide enough to carry you. Come and see, Gromer. Come and see the wide world, and be its master.'

Gromer got off the bed. Or was he still dreaming? He went to the window ledge, and climbed up. Now he was up on the ledge, it was as if he was shrinking. Or was the owl getting bigger? He felt a sudden unease, but the owl whispered, 'Come on, climb on, Gromer, lord of the land of Somer Joure. You will see the world.'

And it bent low so Gromer could more easily climb. Now he was sure he was dreaming, because he could indeed fit on, comfortably. The owl's back was soft and strong, like a dream, and it would carry him far . . .

Tiphaine woke with a start. She'd been having a really bad dream, where she was being dragged through a great pit of dark, and something soft, suffocating, was over her mouth, her eyes, her nose, stopping her from breathing. The panic of it was still strong on her when she opened her eyes – and saw, as if in a dream, a huge owl taking off from the window ledge, with Gromer on its back. She cried out, 'No!' and jumped off the bed.

The great owl turned its head and looked at her, its eyes bright as lamps, full of a laughing intelligence. It said, 'Good evening, Lady Tiphaine,' and then it stepped off the window ledge, into the late golden afternoon, with Gromer sitting, like a carved thing, on its back. She rushed to the window and saw it soaring on the eddies of air, heading towards the woods. She did not stop to think, but flung on dress and cloak, and raced out of the door, down the stairs, through the courtyard, and out into the meadows, running like a mad thing. As bad luck would have it, the rest of the household was busy getting ready for the evening meal, and the only person who saw her go was the youngest of the grooms, who could only say afterwards that he had not even time to call out to her before she had left the safety of the manor and was plunging into the woods. Why she had gone no-one knew; because no-one had seen the owl. No-one except for Lenaik, who was dead; and Estik, who huddled unseen, in an agony of fear, in his fold of curtain, for quite a while after the great bird had flown away, and his charges – the charges Viviane had commended to Estik and his companions – were gone. Only one thought, one tiny comforting thought, helped him: at least Viviane would soon come back, for Penduik would have told her about Rouanez. But the more he huddled and shook, the more the knowledge grew in him that he must do something himself. This was some doing of the korrigans, he was sure of it. It was not Shadow Day, but for some reason, they had breached that custom. He must go to Ti-Korriganed, and see for himself.

Seven

Tiphaine ran and ran, her breath coming fast and burning as the touch of ice in her throat and her chest. She could see the owl, a speck in the distance, and then, once she was in the woods, could hear his passage through the trees ahead of her, and once, even, her brother's voice. She did not wonder at the fact she could see and hear these things, or think she was being lured. She had seen the purpose in the owl's eyes, and known at once it was no natural owl, but a mischief lord from the Otherworld, come to wreak havoc in their lives. She knew what awaited those who went into the world of the korrigans; to go in willingly might very well be fraught with even more dangers than to be snatched. It looked as if Gromer had gone willingly; his voice, when she heard it, sounded excited rather than fearful. The korrigans could be kind to those they took a fancy to, rather as a capricious child may be kind to a pet; but their moods and whims were apt to change very quickly. And besides, she had to know where they were taking him, so she could tell Viviane, so she could help to save him.

The owl was heading for Ti-Korriganed, she realised that very quickly. Her breath caught even more at her throat. But it was not the dangerous time. The really predatory things, the things from the black pit, would not be out and about yet. The owl could not be in league with them. Yet what was a fairy owl, a *korrigantoud*, doing, coming into human chambers and taking children, before Hallowe'en? Usually they were not so bold, before then: they waited for you in places where you were not familiar, when you had lost your way, or followed some fairy song. But then, she had never, ever, seen an owl as big as that one. It was ten times as big as Hopernoz, or any of the other owls she'd ever seen.

Ti-Korriganed loomed up suddenly, the great grey stones rising in the dimming light like huge, cowled shadow-figures. Tiphaine stopped, ice hitting her spine. The owl was sitting by the tallest stone, Gromer standing by it, still with that statue stillness. But there were other creatures around it, at the foot of each stone. Indeed, the whole stone circle was crowded: with what looked at first like birds and animals, but when Tiphaine blinked, resolved into shadowy, insubstantial humanlike creatures, more or less. There were beautiful faces and twisted ones; long limbs and dwarfish stuntedness; red, yellow, blue, green and night-black eyes; long golden hair and green seafronds on round and pointed heads; long ears and little neat ones. All different, yet all curiously with that strange restlessness, that edgy melancholy quick-to-anger that characterised those of the Otherworld. The world of the korrigans.

And the owl – the owl itself, when she saw it that way, was a tall, a very tall man, with bright golden eyes and hair the colour of night, wearing a cloak that looked like owl's plumage, his hands clawed, like those of a bird. He had the bearing of a great lord. Yet she had not heard of a king of the korrigans, hereabouts. Only of Rouanez, and she was a Queen. And *she* was nowhere to be seen.

Tiphaine knew that if she took one more step; if she moved into the shadow of the great stones, she would be in their world, and might not be able to get away. She could still retreat, turn on her heel, flee through the wood back to Raguenel. But Gromer was standing by the korrigan lord, standing so still, and she could not bear that. She stepped forward boldly, and stopped just before the circle of stones.

'Give me back my brother,' she called, in a strong voice. 'He does not belong in your world. And it is not Hallowe'en yet.'

The korrigans turned with a rustling and a whispering to look at her. She felt the combined force of that look, and it crept into her limbs, turning them, as she felt, to stone. But she fought it hard, with all the wild, untutored strength of her mind. 'Give me back my brother. Give me back Gromer.'

The korrigan lord laughed. 'Good evening, Lady Tiphaine.'

'A bad evening to you, sir,' she said, with spirit. 'And may curses descend on you for this unmannerly act. We have always had good relations with the korrigans, we of Raguenel. Give me back my brother.'

'He came willingly with me. To see the world, and be master of it.'

The korrigan crowd flowed and murmured. Tiphaine had a sudden feeling that it was uneasy. She said, 'Lord of the korrigans, you must know there are laws which are obeyed by all. My brother is not rightful prey. Please give him back to me.'

'How can you expect this one to keep to any laws?' The voice, behind her, startled her. She whirled around to see a tall lady coming towards her. Unlike the other people there, she could be seen quite clearly, and cut a vivid figure. Dressed in travelling clothes, with a cloak flung about her, she was beautiful as the night, with very dark hair and eyes the colour of the grass in summer. She had a haughty carriage and an indefinable air about her which made Tiphaine realise this was a very great lady indeed. The Queen, perhaps? She bent her head and said, very humbly, 'Great lady, I beg of you, let my brother go.'

The lady looked expressionlessly at her. She said, with a sudden sharpness in her voice, 'I can do nothing. It was not I he went with. Besides, this much is true. He went willingly.'

'But, my lady—' Tiphaine's eyes filled with tears. 'How have we hurt you?'

'You haven't,' snapped the lady. She stepped briskly away from Tiphaine, and into the circle of stone. The crowd swirled around her. But some stayed closer to the man. Gromer did not move. Tiphaine's eyes stung at the sight of him, so still and lifeless he might as well have been a statue. But the woman was speaking. She was pointing at the man, and there was cold fury in her voice. 'Archduke Bubo, I command you to leave my lands. And leave the boy.'

'No, Rouanez,' said the man, smiling faintly. 'You

know that cannot happen, not now.' He put a hand on Gromer's shoulder. 'The heir of Raguenel came willingly with me.'

The woman stared at him. Her eyes flashed. Then she called out, 'Tiphaine! Come here! Here, I say!'

'No,' said Tiphaine. 'Not until you give me back my brother.'

'You fool,' said the Queen. She marched out of the circle, grabbed Tiphaine by the arm, and pulled her back in. As her feet passed the invisible line that separated Ti-Korriganed from the rest of the wood, Tiphaine felt a shock, a jolt that shuddered all through her. The world shifted, tilted, the air seemed to shatter around her, and then suddenly, the pieces rearranged themselves, the light changed, and she found she was in what looked like a great open courtyard, with pillars of stone all round. Beyond, to one side, she could see a fair country, where it seemed to be spring, or summer, for there were blossoms and fruit everywhere. Around her, the crowd suddenly solidified into proper form, with smells and sounds to match. It was like a picture suddenly brought into focus.

But when she looked back over her shoulder at Stone Wood, all she saw was the kind of half-dark you see before night falls properly, and in that half-light, she saw nothing definite, no real solid shapes, only formless, insubstantial shiftings and murmurings. And by this she knew she had passed the passage into the Otherworld, and the human world was lost to her.

She was brave and bold, Tiphaine, but still a child. The shock of this realisation terrified her, and nearly made her cry, but then she looked up, and saw her brother Gromer, no longer statue-like, but real and living, his eyes seeking hers over the crowd's. Hope began to renew in her heart.

'So, you have the other half, then.' The korrigan lord's amused tones rang across the courtyard of Ti-Korriganed.

'Yes,' said Rouanez. 'So, you see, Bubo, your plan is foiled.'

'Not at all,' said the Archduke. 'It appears we merely have a stalemate, my dear Rouanez.'

'We shall see about that.'

'Not at all. It is easily broken, Rouanez: agree to my terms, as you should have long ago.'

'Never! You are a stranger. You do not belong here. Why didn't you stay in your own country!'

'We were promised to each other, Rouanez.'

'I did not agree. My father made those promises without my consent.'

'Oh, but I waited so long, Rouanez! You did not think I would give up, did you?'

Tiphaine listened in bewilderment, and a growing anger. Finally, she burst out, 'I do not know, my lord and lady, what your quarrels have to do with us! Let us go home!'

'Ah, sorry, no,' said Bubo, and put a hand on Gromer's shoulder again, who flinched. 'You see, my dear little Tiphaine, we are all linked, all of us. We cannot let you go.'

Rouanez's green eyes gleamed like a cat's. 'No, we certainly cannot.'

'Let us revisit this later,' said Bubo. 'When we have both had time to think more clearly.'

Tiphaine tried again. 'What have we got to —'

'Silence!' said Rouanez. She glared at Bubo. 'In five years' time, then. I give you five years to give me a better reason than that you have given me.'

'Very well,' said Bubo, smiling. 'In five years' time.'

Rouanez shouted, 'But if you think you have beaten me, Bubo, by holding Gromer, know that I have Tiphaine. And beauty is a match for strength any day.'

'Is that so?' said Bubo, and in a movement that was almost invisible, he lifted the cloak from his shoulders, and flung it into the air, where it seemed to swoop and hang, like an owl, before descending relentlessly on to Tiphaine, who found herself all at once engulfed in a terrifying deadly softness, turning everything around her black, like in her dream. She fought, and tore at her face to try and free her nose and mouth from the cloak, and managed to pull it away from her, but as she did so, she felt a terrible change come over her, her eyes widening, her nose compressing downwards, her hands recoiling on themselves. She heard a great cry from the crowd, and worse, from her brother Gromer, and knew herself to be immeasurably and hideously changed, her features like a ghastly human parody of an owl. She put her arms around her face, and cried and cried, the tears warmly flowing into her mouth. Then she felt a hand on her shoulder, and Rouanez's voice, no longer angry or haughty, but almost with an edge of tenderness to it, 'Do not cry, Tiphaine. Your beauty never was only of the body.'

Tiphaine sobbed, her transformed head in her hands. 'Can you not take this ugliness from me? Can you not let Gromer and me go home?'

'No. I cannot,' said Rouanez, and for the first time, there was genuine regret in her voice. 'Bubo is a great lord, in our world, and his spell cannot lightly be broken. But I will see what can be done. That is all I can say.'

Tiphaine looked up. Her new owl-eyes stared into Rouanez's with an unblinking intensity. But her voice, and her heart, were unchanged. She looked around her for her brother. But he had gone, as had Bubo: vanished without a sound.

'Where has Gromer been taken?'

'To the Archduke's lands. He will be well looked after. The Archduke would never harm him, he is worth too much to him.'

'He is worth a great deal more to me,' cried Tiphaine, in great agony of mind. 'He is my brother, and I love him.'

'Well, I can do nothing about that,' said Rouanez, uneasily. 'He will be safe, I am sure. And he will not be sad, because he will not remember you, or his old life. He will become a great korrigan warrior, if I know the Archduke Bubo.'

If she thought that was comfort to a human child, she was greatly mistaken. But Tiphaine was brave and resourceful. Even in the midst of her great torment, the thought came to her bright, quick mind that it was not only korrigans who could find out things, not only korrigans who might discover hidden powers. She would be patient. She would not fight any more, not outwardly, but learn as much as she could to free herself and Gromer from their imprisonment.

But in the trees at the edge of Ti-Korriganed, back in the natural world, Estik the nightingale sat with death in his soul. He had found Lenaik's and Hopernoz's bodies; and had just been in time to see Tiphaine vanishing into the stone circle. This was the most terrible day of his life, and would change everything forever.

Eight

*I*n Broceliande, no hint or whisper of what had
happened at Raguenel had reached Viviane,
in her sister's cottage. Her fears for her sister had
been realised as soon as she had come into Nolwenn's
cottage. Nolwenn *was* dying; though she had rallied
a little when she saw Viviane had arrived, she was
inexorably slipping away into the undiscovered
country. She was at the gates of Death. All Viviane
could do was ease her last days with medicines made
from herbs, and hold her hand and talk softly of their
shared childhood, and allow Nolwenn to tell her of her
regrets, of the children she'd borne who had died, of
her husband who was lost at sea, of untaken paths and
unthought decisions. But there was joy in her telling
too, the smell of a life that had been fully-lived.

The priest came a couple of times; he would be there
when the end came. Yet despite the sadness, it was also
a strangely peaceful time for Viviane. Nolwenn was
loved in Broceliande; not only villagers and forest-
dwellers but even the lord's steward had come to visit
her, and Yann de Broceliande himself had sent a basket

of fruit from the manor gardens. The Widow Kemener, Nolwenn's closest friend, was there every day, and far into the night, and though Viviane found her irritating at times, for she was a terrible gossip, and something of a whiner, yet she was also of great help when it came to bathing and tending Nolwenn. There was no doubt of the Widow's devotion; and Viviane found it strangely touching, as well as troubling. Would anyone ever do the same for her?

One morning, Nolwenn received another visitor, the young squire, Bertrand du Gwezklen, bearing a little basket of fresh blackberries and a bottle of cream, which he shoved at the Widow Kemener, mumbling something indistinguishable. Viviane liked him at once, seeing behind the plain face and rough manners to the sweet and fearless heart behind. But the Widow Kemener was much more disapproving.

'You'd be better off bringing your prayers, young man,' she scolded. 'How do you think she can eat such things, in her state?'

Bertrand flushed. 'I thought that—'

'You *don't* think, that is the trouble,' declared the Widow Kemener, snappishly. 'These would have been good weeks ago, when—'

'There would have been no blackberries, then, my dear friend,' said Viviane, gently. 'Come, give them to me. I will make something from them my sister can eat.' She looked at Bertrand. 'Thank you, young man. It is kind of you.'

He flushed even more, and stammered, 'I am ... it is little enough. I ... I just wanted to ... Mistress Nolwenn was kind to me and I—'

'Come, speak to her, it will give her great comfort,' said Viviane and she took his hand and took him right into the back of the cottage, to the curtained bed where Nolwenn lay, peacefully sinking into her last days. His hand in Viviane's was hot and shook a little; yet he came steadily enough. When he reached the bed, he dropped on one knee and spoke in a whisper to Nolwenn, who smiled faintly and whispered back. Viviane left them to it, and made sure the Widow Kemener kept her long nose out of it too by setting her to crush and sieve the blackberries to be combined with the cream and some honey to make a nourishing sweet soup.

After a short while, Bertrand left, after farewelling them all, as awkwardly and shyly as ever, ducking his head and mumbling, then vanishing out of the door with great haste.

'What a clod he is,' said the Widow Kemener, looking after him. 'No wonder, I suppose, with no mother or father to speak of.'

'I do not remember his people,' said Viviane, frowning.

'No, you wouldn't. You had left by the time they came. They came from Gwezklen. They came back with the lord from some foray of his. But they did not last long. The mother died in childbirth – the babe died too, it would've been Bertrand's younger brother, if it had lived – and the father disappeared on campaign. The boy has had to make his own way.'

'He has made it well enough?'

'Hmmm. He is reckoned to be a good fighter. And a hard worker. But like a little wild beast. You saw. He has no idea.'

'Quite the opposite. He seemed to me to have a very good idea,' said Viviane, coldly. 'Nolwenn looked happy to see him.'

Not a bit abashed, the Widow Kemener shrugged. 'Nolwenn was always too kind. I have tried to teach him manners over the years, but he is unteachable. I suppose, if you want a fighter, he's your man. But I cannot see him ever courting a woman. He is ugly as sin, and rough with it. But then, who knows what his parents really were? He is quite ugly enough to be the son of a *ðuz*, of a dwarf.'

Viviane folded in cream and honey with quite unnecessary violence. Her fingers itched to box the Widow's ears. But she desisted. The Widow could not help being born stupid and limited. She truly loved Nolwenn. Perhaps this was part of her way of showing it. And what right had Viviane to argue, when she had left Broceliande years ago?

Yet, later, when she took a break from her vigil over Nolwenn to walk in the woods, she was glad to come across Bertrand in a clearing. He did not appear to see her at first. The young squire was practising his archery; he had rigged up a target against a tree, and was shooting with extraordinary accuracy, and with a natural grace that quite struck Viviane. She stood there for a few moments, watching; then, just as she was about to announce her presence, he said, without turning around, 'Good afternoon to you, Mistress Viviane.'

'Good afternoon, Bertrand,' she said, smiling, unsurprised that she had failed to catch him by surprise.

He picked the arrows from the target, and put them

back in their quiver. She said, 'You are a very good shot, Bertrand. Where did you learn?'

'I have been shooting, and using weapons, most of my life,' he said, and over his plain, young face came a look of almost-old acceptance. 'I am a fighter. That is what I do.'

'Few of us do what we are born to do,' said Viviane, looking steadily at him. 'Even fewer of us know what is in our heart so young.'

'I did not know it was in my heart. It is what I have always been good at.' He looked at her, then at the ground, and scuffed his feet. 'I am sorry, Mistress Viviane, if I . . . if I did the wrong thing this morning. I . . . I do not always know how to act. And the Widow Kemener . . . I am afraid of her,' he added, in a burst of honesty. 'I think she hates me, but I do not know why.'

'You did not do the wrong thing at all. You gave joy to Nolwenn. She loved the blackberries you brought. We made a cream for her; she said it reminded her of the woods. She said it had the very scent of autumn. And as to the Widow Kemener, I do not believe she hates you. She sees something in you that flusters her, that is all. Something rare and extraordinary. And because it flusters her, she tries to shoo it away. So, you see, she has to be sharp with you. Because you frighten her.'

Bertrand laughed heartily at that. But Viviane looked seriously at him, and said, 'Promise me this, Bertrand, that you will never forget to follow your heart. Never allow the scorn or hate or wilful blindness of others make you forget.'

He stopped laughing, and looked back at her. 'I . . . I

am not sure what you mean, Mistress Viviane. But I will try to do as you say.'

'You are a good boy,' she said, smiling, 'not to tell an old woman like me to go about my business.'

'Oh, I would never do that!' he exclaimed. 'You are very kind.' He hesitated a moment. Then, 'Do you ever miss Broceliande where you live, Dame Viviane?'

'Often,' she said, and sighed. 'But I am needed, where I am, and so must stay there till I am no longer needed.'

He nodded, incuriously. He understood about that kind of thing. 'Is it pretty, where you live?'

She smiled. 'Very much so.'

'But not like here,' he suggested, stoutly. She smiled again.

'No. But Raguenel is a beautiful spot. And the people I work for, the Viscount and Viscountess of Raguenel, are good people; their children will, one day, be good and great.' She looked at him, with a sudden intensity. 'They must be about your age, Bertrand. Maybe that is why they remind me of you.'

He nodded politely, thinking, however, that these nobleman's children would be nothing like him.

'Give me your hand,' she said, suddenly, urgently. 'Don't be afraid.'

He stared at her, then gave it to her, shivering a little – for there was a strange fire in her eyes – and she held his hand for a moment. Then she closed her eyes, and traced the lines in it. The hair rose on the back of his neck, stiff and cold, and his belly felt suddenly hollow and aching.

'I see *Ankou*, Mister Death, at your shoulder many a time; grinning at you from many corners; yet you always outface him. I see danger at every turn, and pain, and rejection, and great, great fame. I see Bertrand du Gwezklen at the head of a great army . . . honoured by all . . . but still Ankou grins at you, and false-seeming and illusion try to trap you. But see true, see true, Bertrand du Gwezklen! Beware – beware! Great fame and honour come with a heavy, heavy price.'

Her voice tailed away. She dropped his hand. Her eyes flew open. Her face was very pale. For an instant, she and Bertrand stared at each other. Then he backed away, quietly, his eyes still on her face, his heart hammering so loudly he thought it might leap out of his chest.

Viviane watched him, a strange pain, a sadness gripping at her vitals too. The future rarely came to her in such form; there was so much death, so much pain, so much suffering around this child, and yet such a fiery, glorious greatness it hurt her even to think of it.

She said, softly, 'Bertrand du Gwezklen, your name is not so unlike that of our great poet Gwenc'hlan. And your fame will be like his.'

'Like *Gwenc'hlan*!' That stopped Bertrand. Every Breton knew of the bard who so long, long ago – many hundreds of years ago, when the barbarians had invaded – had sung on the battlefield of the fate of his country. For Gwenc'hlan was not only a bard, but a fighter, too.

'Do you know Gwenc'hlan's song?' said Viviane, gently. He stared at her, and nodded.

'Will you sing it to me?'

He smiled, then. 'I am no songbird, but I will try,' and he raised his voice and began the great song of

Gwenc'hlan. Though he had said he was no songbird, in point of fact he had a pleasant voice, true and clear, and sometimes he had sung with Gwazig, and learnt new tunes from him. But this was an old one, a great ancient song of power, and as he became more involved in the words of Gwenc'hlan, he shut his eyes and let it take him over.

When the sun sets, when the sea swells, I sing on the threshold of my door . . . Oh! When I was young, I sang, now I am old, I sing even more. I sing in the day, I sing in the night, and I sing from sadness. Oh! I can see the boar coming out of the woods, he is lame and limps and bleeds from many wounds, and his muzzle is white with age. Oh! I see the horse of the sea come towards him, white as snow, vast as the ocean, and all the earth trembles . . . Oh! I see the blood on the white, and all the ocean shakes . . .

And then Viviane was joining in, singing with him, and the forest of Broceliande was filled with their song, and all was still around them, as if everything and everyone in Broceliande was listening.

When they had finished, they looked at each other with a little smile, silently, and something like sympathy passed between them, and the shade of Gwenc'hlan himself was bright between them.

Then Viviane came right up to Bertrand, and touched him on the lips, once, twice, three times, with an index finger.

'As it was in his time, so it will be again,' she said, quietly, and her gaze was faraway. 'You say you are no songbird, but you have a gift which will make your life a song to be sung down the ages. Such it is too with my Tiphaine and my Gromer, in Raguenel. Fare thee well,

Bertrand du Gwezklen, and may God watch over you.'

And then she was gone. He did not try to stop her, though he raised a hand in nervous farewell, his guts still churning with the thrill of what she'd said. He went home to his little holding with unaccustomed dreams chasing themselves around in his head.

But as time went on, his practical, modest nature reasserted itself. Whether her sight into the future was true or not, he could not act as if he truly thought he was like Gwenc'hlan. The bard had lived a long time ago, when things had likely been very different. He had likely not been a poor hedge-squire, an orphan boy of no account. And he could only superficially be like Viviane's charges in Raguenel, children of noblemen as they were. Besides, only God knew the truth in these things. It was as well not to trust to fortune-tellings and prognostications, but to take each day as it came.

And when two days later, he was called upon by his lord to leave Broceliande again to take up arms once more, he did so without thinking too much of what Viviane had told him. For he had no way of knowing, that day he left, that he would not see his home again for a very long time, and that nothing in Broceliande would be the same again . . .

As to Viviane, she did not think too much more of Bertrand, or the fate she had seen for him, after that moment. For when she came back to the cottage, she found Nolwenn fading very fast indeed. The weather had suddenly turned by the time Nolwenn died, was properly mourned in a day-long wake, and finally buried. When Viviane set off for Raguenel again, the deceptively mild autumn was transforming into an early wolf-winter, and it took her a long time to get back to the manor. And what she heard there quite banished Bertrand from her mind.

Oh! I am Estik the nightingale, and with my mistress Dame Viviane I roam the world, seeking for news of the lost children!

Alone of my three friends, I roam still, searching, searching!

Lenaik the wren is dead, and Penduik the thrush is lost to the world of the Guardians, and there is only I, to sit on the shoulder of my mistress, and bring her news of far-away places, and forgotten corners of the world!

She is old and worn now, my mistress, for nearly five years she has been looking in all the corners of this world and the world of shadows she can only half see into, and still no sign of the children has she found . . .

I saw Tiphaine in the terrible guise of an owl, and Gromer in the likeness of a stone thing, and our eyes can see neither now, for the korrigans have drawn them back into their realm of darkness! Rouanez does not answer my mistress's calls for mercy, and no other denizen of that world dares to, so we are left to our own resources.

The parents of the children blamed my mistress, in their grief, and they exiled her from Raguenel, and from any other place nearby; and then they closed up the manor, and left never to return.

Still we seek, for the five years of the children's bondage draw to a close, soon, this All Hallows; and then maybe we might see more clearly into the world of the korrigans.

Oh! I am Estik the nightingale, who has already lived too long, who, like my mistress, has lived only so that I may help to wreak vengeance on the korrigans! Not another word will I speak, not another song will I utter, until the children are amongst us again . . .

Part Two

Nine

*T*he water shook and shimmered. Ripples formed underneath, bursting softly as they came to the surface. Silvery bubbles broke; the water smoothed, shook again. Then, at last, the surface was clean, bright, true.

'Well, and not before time!' The *ðuz* shook his head. 'Humans are so slow.' Then he pursed his lips, and his yellow eyes narrowed, as he saw the picture slowly taking shape on the taut mirror-like surface of the water.

Beside him, Tiphaine smiled to herself. She never tired of tricking these tricky creatures; of making them think they knew her, when really . . . Nearly five years in the korrigans' world, and she had come to know *them* very well. Better than they themselves suspected, she thought.

The *ðuz* bent over the picture in the water-mirror. His tongue licked at his lips. He said, softly, 'Beautiful, beautiful . . .'

There was a cave, in the picture. A cave filled with gold. Cauldrons full of it; gold stacked in piles, like drifts of shining leaves, in all the corners; a golden gleam everywhere, like the dearest dream of the most avaricious *duz*. Tiphaine looked at him as he perched oblivious over the water, all his being concentrated on the marvellous picture. She let a little tendril into his mind again, pulling down an image so swiftly and subtly he noticed nothing: a statue, made all of gold. She blinked once, transferring it to the water-mirror. And there it was. The *duz* started, sighed. He clasped his hands. He stared at the water, entranced.

'Where is it?' he whispered.

Tiphaine whispered back, 'In the Archduke Bubo's lands, Gwengan.'

Silence, while he stared at the alluring picture she had made of his deepest desire. Then he said, hoarsely, 'You will tell me exactly where.'

'I cannot. You must take me there, and then I will find it for you.'

So many times, she'd tried this with other *duz*, and with other denizens of the korrigans' world. But until Gwengan, she'd not found one whose inner desire was stronger than his or her fear of Rouanez. Gwengan had spent a great many years in the human world, as the tortured slave of a master sorcerer, and had changed during that time. All *duz* were avaricious; but Gwengan's avarice had become sharpened into something different, a lust for gold that was almost dragon-like in its intensity. Indeed, knowing what she did now, Tiphaine suspected the sorcerer, in his experiments on the hapless *duz*, had somehow injected dragon's blood into the creature's being. Now, the *duz*'s yellow eyes took on a fiery glint as he hissed, 'If you are lying, it will be the worse for you.'

She laughed, mirthlessly. 'Lying? What would be the point, here?'

Gwengan's eyes devoured her face. 'None at all. You are here, and here you stay.'

'So, you don't want the gold, then?' She made a gesture towards the water, as if to dismiss the picture there.

Gwengan broke in, quickly. 'I did not say that.' His eyes swung back to the gold. His ears twitched. His bony hands clenched. She could almost *see* the struggle waged inside his slight frame; the fairy certainty turned to confusion, the ghastly lust for the dead metal burning everything else away in his thin *ðuz*'s heart. Once, she would have been loath to use such a thing, in her quest to be reunited with her brother and free from the korrigans. But she knew now that it was either she and Gromer, or the korrigans. Things she had learnt in recent times had convinced her that Rouanez had no intention of freeing her, when the five years were up; and no intention of helping to secure Gromer's freedom from Bubo, either. Like the sorcerer, they'd have to be forced to give up their prey, by whatever means was possible. The sorcerer had paid in the end with his life, for what he'd done to Gwengan, when the creature had finally turned on him. The korrigans could not be killed, but they could be rendered helpless. She waited.

'Very well.' The *ðuz*'s voice was very soft, his eyes reflecting back from the mirrored piles of gold. 'I will take you there.'

'When?'

He shivered suddenly, as if a cold wind had brushed at the nape of his neck. But Tiphaine, her heart leaping into her mouth, knew that meant one of Rouanez's most feared spies was not far away; one of the long-fingered, cold-eyed, dead-faced, thin-bodied air-korrigans that could come upon you as silently, and invisibly, as a breath of winter air. Gwengan knew it too, of course. He said, crossly, 'When you learn how to make water-pictures properly, then might be the time to take you to see Her Majesty again,' and he picked up a stone and skimmed it at the water, breaking the mirror-picture and shattering Tiphaine's concentration. But she knew he had done the right thing. His unnatural lust for gold was ringed around with a protective duplicity; it made him both cunning and fearless in that one area.

Tiphaine bent her head, as if in acknowledgement of reproof. The cold wind lingered an instant at her back, as well at Gwengan's, then moved on. The spy must have been satisfied that what she had overheard was of no consequence. But what of the picture? Had she seen the picture in the water? Tiphaine hoped not; if what she had thought was true, then Gwengan's true heart had only been seen by her, because of the way he had been corrupted from his stay in the human world. Thus, the korrigans could only ever guess at her own true feelings; but that did not matter to them. They did not care how she felt, only that she could not escape. It was only slowly that she had come to understand that in that blindness lay her best hope.

How to describe what had happened to Tiphaine in the korrigans' country? In some ways, she had not been unhappy; she had even grown to accept the sight of her own hideously transformed shape. For in this place, there was no one shape which could be called hideous; the Otherworld was so bewilderingly diverse in the forms and bodies of its denizens that Tiphaine could easily count more than a hundred different shapes all more bizarre than hers. And if the pain of ugliness is to know you are different from others, that you somehow transgress against the notion of beauty by your very existence, then such a thing was unknown in the world of the korrigans. Here none was ugly to anyone else, but just *was*, without qualification. Though it was the realm of Beauty itself, though nothing in that world decayed or grew old, ugliness to them was a thing of no consequence. Oh, they knew well enough that in the human world, Tiphaine's transformation would have caused her to be shunned by her fellow humans, to have children throw stones at her, even: and that was how she might also be kept here, indefinitely, at their pleasure; but her ugliness meant as little to them as her beauty would have done, except as a bargaining chip. And yet strangely that had helped to strengthen Tiphaine's secret, dearly-held resolve to escape that place.

Yet the country of the korrigans was beautiful, and pleasant enough, with sparkling streams, soft orchards, clean, neat and pretty manors. The days were always sunny here; yet the springs and rivers flowed merrily, and the grass was like green velvet, as if it had been watered by countless rain-showers. As to the nights, they were soft and perfumed and warm.

Tiphaine had come to understand that Rouanez's realm was only one province, one kingdom, amongst many other such little states in *mabrokorr*, the korrigan world: and Archduke Bubo's was another such state, at present a rival to Rouanez's kingdom. It was perpetual early summer in *mabrokorr*, with flowers and fruit, together, on every tree; crops grew without having to be tended, and the korrigans spent their days in idle pursuits, eating, drinking, riding, singing, telling stories, playing music, and the occasional shrieking quarrel.

Tiphaine had been included in most of these things, apart from the quarrels. But even a well-treated prisoner cannot forget she is in custody. She had been looked after as well as the korrigans knew how, without any of the human warmth that might have made it bearable. She had plenty to eat and drink, all with that ineffable fairy taste that left her longing for something juicier, earthier, richer in taste and texture. She was never alone, but had various korrigans and *duzig* assigned to her as companions and guards, and sometimes these taught her scraps of fairy lore, or song, or of little bits of magic. They were friendly enough; but would soon tire of her and ask to be transferred, and then forget her completely, so with no denizen of this world had she ever developed anything like a real friendship.

Sometimes, too, Rouanez herself would call her into her fragrant bower and allow her glimpses of her brother, through the pictures brought back by spies; but never once did she feel that the korrigan Queen cared about her. She hardly even called Tiphaine by her real name; addressing her mainly as 'Ragnell-girl'. Yes, to Rouanez, 'Ragnell-girl' was just a pastime and a pawn in this strange game the Queen was playing with Archduke Bubo. Quite what the game entailed, Tiphaine was still not sure; only that it was a contest of wills between two determined adversaries.

She had been here nearly five years now. But she knew this only because she had overheard Rouanez talking to one of her councillors of how the years were almost up. Otherwise, she would have been hard pressed to know. Time passes differently in the Otherworld, sometimes faster, sometimes slower, than in the human world. Korrigans, like all the fairy kind, live in an eternal present. Not like animals, who have no notion of past and future though their lives progress inexorably from birth to death; more like angels, who see all time together. Both korrigans and angels are immortals. The past and future only exist as real markers for human beings, who mourn the loss of loved ones and things, and hope for change.

However, unlike angels, korrigans cannot see the end of time itself, only that one day it will end and they will pass with it, so they are both less powerful and less fearsome, but also more whimsical and unpredictable, even cruelly so, than the angels, who are true immortals. In their unchanging country of *mabrokorr*, which lies within and beside the human world, the korrigans know that one day everything will end for them. Knowing no hope, they also know no fear.

And for one brought into their world, that lack of fear can be a powerful thing. It can arm a human heart against many things, especially if that human heart is a fine one to begin with, like Tiphaine's. For others, it can be a deathly thing, that strange country known to many in the human world as the hollow lands. There are those who have been sent mad by a single night spent in the company of the korrigans; and others whose weaknesses have been targeted by the whimsical things and tortured to a kind of living death.

No, Tiphaine had not been treated unkindly, if you discounted prying eyes and whispering tongues. That went with korrigans. Watching was their second nature; that, and jumping out at you suddenly. Curiosity is very strong in korrigans. Those sharp-featured faces were often alight with the glee of secret knowledge. But they did not always use the knowledge; sometimes, it seemed to be enough to hoard it. They were curious about humans: every square inch of Tiphaine had been prodded and poked by curious fingers. Though korrigans had little understanding of human passions except what they'd gleaned second-hand from their occasional captives and hostages, they knew that in this, fairies of all sorts did differ from humans. And it fascinated them. But they could see a person's *daouden*, or their doubleman, as they called it, very well. In our world, we sometimes call those things souls, or spirits, or presences. But only in *mabrokorr* could a *daouden*'s form be properly seen. When humans were in their own world, the korrigans could only apprehend the *daouden* as a kind of shimmering mist. And of course most humans never saw it at all, in or out of their own world, though they can often be sensed by other people.

Apart from korrigans, only those humans with the sight could see *daoudens* by people's side. *Daoudens* looked just like their bodied people, and were never seen separately from them, unless that person was about to die a violent or unexpected death. Then the *daouden* might sometimes appear separately to Sighted people, as a warning.

The only humans who did not appear to have a *daouden*, Rouanez told Tiphaine, were those who had gone mad as a result of korrigan interference, or who had interfered with the korrigans or other beings of the Otherworld. In these people, the *daouden* had retreated to unreachable corners of the multi-dimensional universe, sometimes even in *mabrokorr*, and might only rejoin their fleshy companions in the moment just before death.

And sometimes, though very rarely, there was the odd person who had permanently given up their *daouden* to the forces of darkness in return for power, whether temporal or magical. These people were even feared by the korrigans themselves: such had been the sorcerer who had enslaved Gwengan. But because they were human, even these ones could not long support the weight of darkness itself, which ate like a cancer at their attenuated selves.

Korrigans themselves had no *daouden*, any more than they had shadows or reflections, though they might seem like shadows and dreams themselves when they passed into the human world. In their own world, though, they had a very strong form, a material firmness that was nevertheless fluid like water. In fact, they were more elemental than solid, in all ways. Their very elusiveness made their force. You could not see the wind, but it nevertheless uprooted trees and destroyed buildings; you could not hold water in your hands, but it nevertheless triumphed over great fleets. And their magic was of that kind too: not learned spells and occult alphabets, but sharp, quick, sudden flashes, surprising gifts and terrifying curses, though they loved words and music and often made binding things with them. If they hated anything, it was the desire of humans to tame that magic.

Tiphaine had learnt that quickly. Bright and sharp herself, she could almost have had a spot of korrigan quicksilver blood herself, according to Rouanez, who from time to time expressed her intention to check on that once and for all. But a typical korrigan laziness – or sheer lack of motivation, rather, in most things – prevented the Queen from following up her genealogical intention. She was preoccupied with her game of oneupmanship with Archduke Bubo, and Tiphaine was of interest only insofar as she was perhaps a useful counter to the boy Bubo had captured. Rouanez had forgotten, if she'd ever really taken it in for more than a fleeting instant, just what Tiphaine felt about her brother; he was only 'the other human creature' to her. She was determined that her own country should surpass in prestige and honour and cleverness everything Bubo might devise.

But the Queen's interest in Gromer's progress, and how Bubo was going to use him against her, had been a very great blessing for Tiphaine. For Rouanez's air-spies brought back frequent news of what was happening there: news which was not just retold, but *shown*. This was news captured, as it were, from the very ether, rolled into the tightly-woven spiderweb-silk bags carried by the spies, and unrolled again at the other end to display living moments of Gromer's existence in Bubo's lands. So bright and lifelike were these captured moments that Tiphaine could hardly refrain from crying out with the pain and joy of it. In the beginning, in fact, she had cried out, jumped forward, tried to take the pictured, living, moving Gromer in her arms; only to meet with the cold embrace of the silken spy-web, and the laughter of the watching korrigans. She had learnt to school herself now, not to show anything when the webbed moments were unrolled; but each sight of Gromer, growing in stature, in strength, no longer a boy but now a man, was like a dagger of yearning in her breast. And each time had strengthened her own resolve that one day they would be together again. He had grown tall and strong, Gromer, with large, powerful chest and shoulders; he was, as Rouanez had predicted, being turned into a great warrior, while Tiphaine was being desultorily schooled in the subtle ways of korrigan cleverness. Tiphaine had already seen some of his feats of arms, and been so sorrowfully proud of him. She thought that Bubo must have his own air-spies, that Gromer must be watching his sister's life too in little rolled-up, spied-on moments, and that he must be feeling the same thing . . .

She had puzzled through ways of trying to reach him. She had tried sending him pictures from her mind, but they had bounced back, as from a wall. She had thought of bribing one of the air-spies; but one moment's real brush with one had taught her instantly that a stone might be easier to persuade. She had tried to appeal to Rouanez's mercy, but the korrigan Queen had looked at her uncomprehendingly. She had tried making magic mirrors, infusing them with her own desires, but all they had ever shown her were confused and hallucinatory pictures which at first she did not understand, but finally came to realise were the stray thoughts and dreams of humans beyond the korrigan world. The desires and thoughts of strangers! It was thus that she had come to realise that alone of the *ðuz*, Gwengan's mind was actually approachable in that

way. She had not been sure how she could use that
knowledge to help Gromer and free herself; but now,
she was groping towards a solution.

Ten

$\mathcal{T}$he wood was filled with threatening noise, cries, shouts, screams, swearing. The pale crescent moon navigated slowly through a thick island archipelago of dark-blue cloud, lighting the wood only fitfully.

Bertrand hunkered down in the undergrowth, hardly daring to breathe. He had lost most of his companions; in their headlong flight after the ambush they had become separated from him, though he had tried to yell at them to come back. He could hear the English crashing around near him, looking for the scattered remnants of the band. He clutched on to his sword. He would sell his life dearly, if need be!

In the last few years since he'd left Broceliande, the war had become fiercer; the bewildering clash of loyalties and shifts of allegiance had meant that at any one time in the woods and forests were at least three and, sometimes, more forces. It was hard to tell who was allied with whom; whether the English, the Scots, the Burgundians, the Bretons, the French, the Gascons and others were friends or allies or enemies that week.

Anarchy had descended on the countryside; bands of lawless men roamed, their allegiance more to their stomachs and their purses than to any prince's standard. Many peasants had left their villages and their crops to flee into the woods, where at least they could build small fortified places. Whole villages had been laid to waste; people were hungry in the cities as a result. And above the heads of the suffering population, the Wolf and the Bull and the Lion and all the other princes slugged it out, with the Breton Ermine running between their feet, nipping and shrieking.

It wasn't only in Brittany that such a dire situation lay heavy, however; other provinces and counties were being ripped apart as well. Bertrand knew this because after the death of his Lord, Yann de Broceliande, he had served in many different groups of armed men over the last few years; and everywhere was suffering and confusion, as well as advantage for the cunning, the ruthless, and the profiteering. There were those who grew fat on the suffering of others; who would turn in their only child or aged grandparent, if it might increase the wealth in their coffers. And there were those who loved war above all because of the opportunities it gave for killing others without being punished for it.

Bertrand had quite lost any illusions he might once have had, about the ultimate goodness of human nature; not that he'd ever had many. He had long accepted that each one of us had been created with the potential for both good and evil within us. Devil and angel both had a place in a person's soul and which one would dominate depended on a person's capacity for struggle. No-one could pretend the struggle was easy, or obvious;

sometimes the devil had a fair face, the angel a harsh one. Bertrand knew this to be true in himself, as well as in others. In recent years, he had become sadder; sadder, and yet more determined. There had to be a better way to solve these quarrels than this endless and futile war.

An idea had taken root in his hard little head a year or so ago: a sense that instead of simply going where he was told by those who had bought his individual sword, he would create a band of fighters himself. Partly, the idea was inspired by conversations with a footloose French cleric he'd met in the north who'd told him how the Romans had fought. Partly it had come from his own observations. He dreamed that his band of fighters could become the nucleus of a real army. They would be well-disciplined, clever, they would never loot or pillage or engage in pointless skirmishes, but would be ruthless, if they needed to be. If this worked, he'd put himself and his band at the service of a far-sighted lord who thought of greater goals than mere point-scoring and vendetta. Who that lord would be he had no idea. Of one thing only was he certain. Strategy was needed, if the country was ever to have real peace again, and he could return to his little holding in Broceliande.

Something had to hold people together, other than the wish to enrich themselves, or the need for individual glory.

But having an idea and carrying it out are two very different things. Especially if the people you try to persuade of the wisdom of your plan are so used to changing horses in mid-stream that it is second nature to them.

In recent weeks in these western woods, Bertrand had managed to gather around him a group of young men, disaffected like himself. He had tried to drill them into some semblance of unity, as well as teach them the tactics he'd learnt in his years fighting for others and his knowledge of the woods.

Whilst they were training, it seemed to work; but, alas! as soon as the real thing happened – as soon as they were ambushed by a party of English, everything he'd tried to instil in them had flown to the four winds. They were not cowards, far from it; they fought hard and strong, but each man fought for himself, and all too quickly the combination of surprise and individuality had broken the back of the 'unit' completely. There had been chaos. Many had taken to their heels, fleeing to live and fight another day; some had no doubt been killed; others captured; others were even now being chased through the woods by the victorious English, or 'Goddamns', as they were popularly called, on account of their constantly using the swearwords 'God damn!'

The worst of it was that the Goddamns themselves had hardly operated as a disciplined unit; and so failure had been particularly galling for Bertrand.

Now, alone, he hunkered down in his hiding-place, cursing and fuming. *Mallozh Doue*! he muttered furiously to himself, *Good God*! Why did you give me such a bunch of useless beginners to go with! But he knew inside that the fault lay not in his men, and certainly not with God, but in and with himself. It was he who had let them down, not the other way around. Perhaps he was too young, too ugly, too short, too poor, to inspire the kind of emotion a commander needed to instil in his men. Or perhaps he was just too useless.

He hit at his forehead. Perhaps he'd just better accept things as they were and go and sell his sword to the highest bidder. Everyone else did, these days; feudal and clan loyalties dissolving in this anarchy. Meanwhile . . .

He waited a few moments while the cries and crashing died away. He did not want to be captured by the Goddamns, but he owed it to his band to at least try and find survivors and bury those who had died. It was the least he could do, before going back into his appointed servitude as a futile fighter in a futile war.

His heart was heavy as he crawled out from his hiding place. He made his silent way through the undergrowth, reconstructing the path his men had taken as they fled or fought.

Mallozh Doue! There was poor Yannik, dead as mutton; the wood would never resound to the merry sound of his little reed, ever again. Bertrand knelt beside the fallen youth, gently closed his staring eyes, and said a prayer for the repose of his soul. Then he pulled the body carefully to one side, covering it with leaves and twigs; he would return with help once he'd found everyone who could be found. And he'd find a priest to conduct a proper Mass, later.

Grimly, he went on. A few short paces later, he came across the sprawled body of another man, Bernard, a grizzled veteran of the war who'd hardly spoken more than two words in all the time he knew him. Further on was yet another dead man, but when he turned him over he saw it was not one of his, but a Goddamn. No matter; a man was a man, and not to be left to the mercies of wild beast. For this man, too, Bertrand performed a few sketchy rites, and pulled him next to Yannik and Bernard. He went on. No more bodies for a good long while; and Bertrand's spirits rose slightly. The battle had seemed fierce enough, but had it been deceptive in its ferocity?

Now he came closer to the ambush place itself: and saw that the Goddamns were there in full force, milling around excitedly, laughing amongst themselves, obviously the conquerors of the hour. None of Bertrand's men were with them: except for one, the youngest member of the band, Alain Mabig, or Little Alan. Alain was called thus not just because of his age, but his stature: he was even shorter than Bertrand, almost of dwarfish proportions, and thin as a whip as well. At nearly sixteen, Alain was just under two years younger than Bertrand himself, and an orphan like him. Unlike Bertrand, though, Alain was not hardened to the realities of the world; his main characteristic was an amazing musicality, and a sweetness that made him seem even younger than he was.

Bertrand's fists clenched. He owed it to Alain not to leave him to the Goddamns' mercies. Not that those mercies would be any worse than if the captors had been French or Burgundians or Scots or whoever else might choose to blunder around in these woods.

But Alain's narrow little face was full of misery, his darting green eyes had lost their merriment, his wrists were tied with rope, his thin shoulders were hunched timidly in his bloodstained tunic as if he expected to be flogged at any moment. He was scared stiff, poor lad; this had been his first experience of fighting.

He'd persuaded Bertrand to take him on, one day,

when he'd met him in the courtyard of a manor-house. He was without family, friends, work or home, he'd said; children threw stones at him because he was a stranger: please, please, take me with you! And now he was being led off into imprisonment, teased and manhandled by a rough Goddamn with great big shoulders and a powerful roar of a laugh. An imprisonment that might in his case last forever; for who would ever ransom him? That was a part of the livelihood of warrior bands, ransoming mummy's boys and merchants' offspring and sometimes even the children of lords, caught in ambushes. But those who had no wealthy relatives to call on, or devoted family to petition for them, would usually either become the servants of such bands – or more accurately, slaves – or, if they were big and strong enough, or showed particular aptitude, simply be inducted into the band itself, never to return home. That is, if they didn't die of hunger or cold or from the plague, or in a battle.

And a little creature like Alain – what had he been thinking of, letting himself be persuaded by the boy in the first place – stood about as much chance of surviving as an icicle in a fire. And yet, he must have fought bravely. If he alone had been captured, and only Yannick and Bernard were dead, then that meant the others must have got away. Once the coast was clear, they might return ... Or they might not. Who knew what would happen, in these strange and desperate times?

Bertrand shook himself. He measured the distance between himself and the Goddamns, turned over possibilities in his mind, and finally came to the only conclusion he could. There was no point trying to spirit

Alain away now; he'd simply become another captive himself, for he was vastly outnumbered. He'd have to wait until the roistering Goddamns settled down for the night. They'd have to sleep soon; the dawn was not very far away, and the battle had been a lively and wearing one.

So once again, he settled down to wait, his mouth set in a grim line, his stomach churning with the mixed emotions of the day.

Time passed. The crescent moon had long since vanished, swallowed up into the dark ocean of the wolf-hour sky, but still the Goddamns kept up their singing and shouting, clustered cosily around the fire they had lit. They did not seem to be treating their captive badly; indeed, they had untied his wrists, and given him roast meat and mugs of beer or whatever it was they had with them. In his dark corner, Bertrand could almost envy Alain. He felt an immense, treacherous weariness stealing into him, like a thief robbing you of valuables. His eyelids kept trying to swoop on to his eyes like hawks on prey; his limbs were melting like honeycomb on a hot day, his mouth was stiff as stone. He would fall into the pit of sleep soon; he could only feebly grapple at the edges of it as he . . .

Hola! He was wide awake, suddenly, as if freezing water had been dashed over him. But it was not water or anything like it that made the back of his neck prickle, and the hair rise stiffly on the head. It was the sound of a voice, singing. A clear, high, silvery voice, trilled with an edge of darkness. The voice of Alain Mabig! And the song, too, Bertrand knew: it was the song known in Brittany as 'The March of Arthur'; a

94

wild battle-song that called all men to it, but was also a lament for the dead and for the loss of land and peace.

Come, come, let us go to battle! Come, come, brother, father, son, cousin, let us go, all men of great heart! They say there are men on the mountain; men in the forest and men on the sea: they are coming to take us, and they are mounted on grey horses that snort and puff out cold air! Come, come, let us go to battle! Oh, come, brother, father, son, cousin, men of great heart! Here is Arthur, mounted on his charger, and there beside him, the men of his army: oh, let us come! Let the valleys be filled with blood, for the blood that has been spilt!

Bertrand could see the boy, standing straight and small in front of the fire, head flung back, singing; and around him, all the Goddamns had fallen quiet. The song was carried clear through the woods; Alain sang like one possessed, like a man who is half-korrigan in the strange haunting magic of his voice. Tears had sprung unheeded to Bertrand's eyes; a cold, thrilling sadness iced his veins, and he knew without having to look that all the other men there were gripped by the self-same thing, the mixture of furious joy and wild melancholy that is at the base of so many fighting men's hearts. Even if they could not understand the Breton words, it did not matter; they were all brothers, suddenly, in that instant of song. It would wake in them both the urge to battle more, and the desperate yearning for their own homes and hearths, that haunting song, sung in the child's high, clear, dark-edged voice.

Around them, the trees had stopped their shifting murmur of leaves; the sky plunged high and thickly dark above them; the wildlife of the woods was utterly quiet. A strange little quirky thought seemed to hit at Bertrand's backbone like an arrow from a bow: a feeling that the song, somehow, was opening a window, slicing through the thin world like a knife cut into flesh. A window of time, of space: a space of . . . what? Shivers rippled up and down him; he thought, this song – this song, it will attract the korrigans. It will call them from their world, it will make them steal into the corners beside me, they will be watching, listening . . . listening . . .

Eleven

*R*ouanez shot out a hand and gripped Tiphaine's wrist.

'Listen . . . listen—'

Tiphaine had been on her way to make arrangements with Gwengan, away from prying ears and eyes. She jumped, heart hammering, at the Queen's silent approach. 'Listen to what, Your Majesty?'

Rouanez pulled down Tiphaine by the hair, and whispered into her ear, 'Your *daouden* knows: it is bending to the sound. Listen . . . it is the voice of a lost one, calling to us from the world—'

'A lost one?' Tiphaine's heart gave another leap. 'My brother?'

'No, you fool! A lost one in the world!' Rouanez's icily beautiful face was full of a strange fire, her eyes glittered. 'Look into my eyes, and listen—'

Tiphaine looked, though it was her instinct not to. At first, she saw only the glitter of fairy eyes, the glint which is like the sparkle of water, and fire. And then, quite suddenly, she saw, and heard . . .

A child, a little taller than a duz *but not a great deal more, standing by a fire, singing. Around him, faces reflected in firelight, like fugitive reflections caught in a dream. Faces of men; some comely, some rough, a few mutilated or surly, but all with a strange look glazed over their features like a transparent veil. A yearning, a pain, a need. Tiphaine shivered. The song resonated in her, too; her skin jumped with the effect of it. If for those in the human world, it was as if an injured star had come down to earth, its silver radiance bleeding over the darkly familiar things, for Tiphaine it brought back warm-scented memories of the earth, of her own home, of all that she missed and loved and longed for with all her heart. She watched and listened, as the music rolled on and on. She could see the faces a little more clearly; the boy's face, narrow, with closed eyes in the ecstasy of song. And suddenly, just beyond him, in the darkness, something else, another face, glimpsed in only a fraction of a second: a young man's face, strong, plain, with small, bright eyes, a firm mouth. The eyes turned to her . . . they opened wide in a huge surprise, which she read as fear and horror, and for an instant, she saw her own hideously metamorphosed face reflected back to her in the young man's eyes. With a little cry, she turned her own face away, quickly, pain gripping at her, and then the song ended, the firelight vanished, the faces, the boy, everything . . .*

'Mine,' whispered Rouanez, 'he must be mine—' The korrigan Queen's face was contorted with desire and yearning. 'Bubo must not be allowed to have him . . . to see him—'

Tiphaine stared at her uncomprehendingly. She shook her head to try and clear it. She felt immensely weary, as if she'd been running for miles. Her very bones ached. The song was still in the fibres of her ears; she could have wept with the need to be back in the world. But then she remembered the look of horror and fear on the face of the man who had been watching in the shadows, and this time could not even weep with the bitter sorrow of the knowledge that for her fellow-men now, she was a monster, one who could not be seen in earthly daylight or night without loathing. She put up a hand to her face, feeling the soft feathery skin, the leathery mouth, the broken nose she was used to, with a renewed despair. She was a monster. Even if she freed Gromer, she could never return with him to the human world. Never . . . never . . . *never* . . . The word tolled like a knell in her heart.

'And you will go!' said Rouanez, triumphantly, turning to Tiphaine, and gripping her wrist again. The girl started.

'Go where?'

'Out there!' The korrigan Queen waved her arms about. 'You and Gwengan; you seem to be getting on well. I'm going to send you into the *mabroden* – the world of the humans – to find that boy and bring him to me. He is a lost one. He belongs here!'

Tiphaine stared at her. Rouanez frowned. 'What's the matter? I thought you would be happy to be out in the human world, the *mabroden*! Mind you, you can't stay there: not that anyone would have you there; but with you *and* the boy, I can't lose! Cleverness and music, together! What is a warrior beside that? Bubo will have to announce himself beaten!'

'Your Majesty,' said Tiphaine, very quietly, for she knew from experience how quickly the korrigan could go from bright to dark, 'I do not understand why I should be the one to—'

'Agh, Ragnell-girl, you are a fool, sometimes! My kind and I can only come into *mabroden* unscathed at certain times and in certain places; and this place where this boy is, was ringed by a spell sometime ago, as you should know!' Her lips curved into a cruel smile. 'Didn't you recognise that place? No, perhaps not, you human things are blind at night, are you not? It is in a wood . . . a wood in *mabroden* that you know well—'

'Stone Wood . . .' whispered Tiphaine, her eyes on Rouanez's face. The Queen nodded, casually. 'Is that what you call it? Yes. That *strobinella* – that Guardian woman, Viviane – she put a curse on it, when she came back to find you had disappeared. It is a binding, that stops us going past the stone ring—'

Tiphaine put a hand to her heart. She stammered, 'Viviane? Where is she now—'

'She is still looking for you,' said Rouanez dryly. 'With that motheaten nightingale on her shoulder. Much good may it do her. She is far away from that place, anyway, so do not even imagine you can find her. But she has barred me and my kind from that place; we have been able only to reach Ti-Korriganed. The rest is locked, barred.'

A sudden, wild hope and fury flared in Tiphaine's heart. But she said nothing.

'So you and Gwengan will go in; you can go, because you are human, even if the humans won't know it; and Gwengan, having been in the sorcerer's power, is not fully korrigan any longer. You will go in, find the boy, entice him to come with you, in whatever way you can think of, I don't care. You will return with him – and you *will* return,' she added, 'because I am giving you seven days and seven nights to do this; and on the eighth night, know I am to meet Bubo at Ti-Korriganed, and you, Ragnell-girl, and the youth Bubo holds, your brother, will be there too. If you do as I say, I may well find a way to free you and your brother. If you do not – if you try to escape, or to frustrate me in any way – your brother will never, ever come out of *mabrokorr*; and you will never ever lose the hideous shape you are in, but will be condemned to live in it in *mabroden* forever, and never be allowed to come even into *mabrokorr* again. Is that clear?'

Tiphaine's heart bled, but she nodded, dumbly.

'Good. Now, we had better arrange for you to wear a mask, or you will frighten the child. And I don't want him to know who you are, not until he is well out of *mabroden*. He has been lost; and so he may have forgotten.'

'Forgotten?'

Rouanez exclaimed, impatiently, 'Are you being dim on purpose, or is it just your human blood, overwhelming any blessed tint of korrigan you might have had? He is lost, Ragnell-girl, because he *belongs* here. He is one of us. He is a korrigan child, lost somehow in *mabroden*. Maybe he had a human father or mother; no matter. So did my friend Merlin. I need a child, a son, if I am to forestall Bubo's ambitions; and he will be just right.'

'But—' Tiphaine began, then closed her mouth. What was the use of saying to the korrigan Queen that the child, whoever he was, might not want to leave his friends and go into a strange land, with two strange creatures like herself and Gwengan? If the child truly had korrigan blood, he might well react like the korrigans themselves, with sharp, shallow curiosity and a lack of love or loyalty. And if he did not: well, she would come to that when she knew it, if she ever did. She had no option. She had to do as Rouanez wanted her to.

But inside, deep inside her soul, where the *daouden* lived, hope grew, quietly, bright and questing. Rouanez saw it, as she saw the *daouden*; but as she lived without hope herself, she had no idea how it might help or hinder. It was a superfluous thing, for a korrigan; and so she could set it aside. The Ragnell-girl would be back, she was sure of that; she was intelligent, and would find a way both to bring the lost one back, and know that she had no choice but to return. She was far too attached to her brother not to do so.

Twelve

W hat had he seen! God in Heaven, what had that face been, leering at him out of the darkness! Bertrand crossed himself. The thing had not looked like any korrigan he'd ever heard of. Was it a demon? A demon attracted by the sound of Alain Mabig's voice? The sight had filled him with a kind of horror.

Yet there had been something else in those terrible eyes, something that disturbed him much more: the eyes of a soul in torment. Perhaps it was indeed that: not a demon, but a damned soul. A soul, condemned to eternal regret and horror, trying to draw close to the old world, the world of humans. Unexpected tears sprang into his eyes. Poor thing. Poor, poor thing . . .

He shivered, and shook himself. Such imaginings did no good. The face had gone, and he had work to do. The song finished, Alain fell silent, and so did the Goddamns. Their exuberance quenched by the power of the song, they were settling down to sleep, quietly. Bertrand watched them for quite a while. He tried to empty his mind and heart of everything but what he had to do. There would be sentries left to watch, but at the edges of the clearing. He had to try and get into the heart of the group by the fire, where Alain and the other captives lay with their cloaks rolled around them.

Strangely, he no longer felt tired. Alain's song, and then seeing that face in the darkness, had acted on him like a douse of cold water.

At last, when he was sure almost everyone in the makeshift camp was asleep, apart from two sentries who sat close together, talking softly, Bertrand crept from his hiding place. On his belly, he crawled towards the sleeping group. It was very dark now, for the moon had set, and it would be very difficult for even very alert sentries to see him. And he was well-schooled in not being heard.

Closer he came, closer, until he was close enough to touch the Goddamn who lay closest to Alain. Bertrand's glance took him in briefly: he was a young man a little older than himself, with a shock of fair hair that hid his face. He had one arm outflung in sleep, pinning down Alain, who was fast asleep too. Closer still, and Bertrand reached over, and gently touched Alain's shoulder.

The boy's eyes opened straight away. They widened when he saw Bertrand, who put a finger to his mouth. Alain's eyes widened again. Bertrand could see he understood at once. Gently, he shifted a little from under the Goddamn's sleeping grasp, trying to break free of the arm without alerting the man. Bertrand retreated a little, watching. Once Alain had wriggled free, they would wake the other captives, and steal away. All was going well; it was as if the lingering spell of Alain's song still lingered there, holding the whole clearing in a timeless moment. Bertrand shook his head as the thought came to him. A little unease crept under his skin. Surely, things were going almost too well ... He held his breath, willing Alain to hurry. There he was, there, now, slipped successfully from under the constraining arm. He straightened up carefully, flashed a grin at Bertrand, who gave him the thumbs-up, and motioned for him to fall back towards the line of trees. Alain nodded, quickly, then stepped delicately away from the tumbled group of men, backing towards the shadows. Bertrand watched him for an instant, a little anxiously, but proudly too. Suddenly, he felt a light touch on his leg. Suppressing the urge to spin around, he turned carefully – to see the Goddamn who had been sprawled near Alain, sitting up, eyes wide.

For a long instant, it seemed, they stared into each other's eyes. Neither of them moved. No-one else woke up. Bertrand's hand stole to his side, to the sword he always wore. The stranger stared at him; then, without a word, he pointed into the shadows. His eyes were still wide with a kind of horror, a fear that seemed to have nothing to do with being unarmed. Bertrand's skin crept again, his heart thumped. Somehow, he knew this was no trick. He turned his eyes slowly towards the shadows; and saw the shadows shifting and tumbling, and Alain writhing in the grasp of two beings whose form seemed made of the night itself. He could not see them clearly, only that one was short and squat; and that the other was twisted, crooked, deformed in some hideous fashion. Between them, the boy was like a beam of silver light, being swallowed by darkness.

Bertrand did not hesitate, though his blood beat loudly in his ears as he remembered the demonic vision he had seen. He jumped away from the camp, and ran towards the shadows, his sword drawn. There was a flurry of movement, a desperate scurry, and the shadows shifted away, Alain between them, behind the line of trees and into the wood, away from the clearing. Bertrand raced after them; and then he heard footsteps crackling behind him, and a voice, panting, 'Quick, quick . . . it's no good just drawing the sword, you can't use it on them, stop, hold it up like a cross . . . yes . . . hold it hilt-up, say these words, *Twylyth Teg, begone and leave us alone —*'

The Goddamn was just behind him, at his shoulder, talking volubly, in a strange kind of tongue that was like Breton yet not, understandable to the other youth yet strangely foreign too. Bertrand gave him one startled glance; then did as he was told. He held his sword up like a cross, and muttered not the strange words the Goddamn had told him, but a Breton charm against the korrigans.

'Ha!' said a harsh voice. 'That's no good against us, you fools. We're proof against it.'

'It's no good,' whispered another voice, sweet and sorrowful, it seemed to Bertrand, though surely that could not be so. 'It's no good, friends. There is nothing to be done —'

'You've stopped,' said the Goddamn, in that odd accent of his. 'That's enough for now.'

'Ha! You fool! Do you know with whom you meddle?'

'We do,' said Bertrand, after a glance at the other man. 'You are creatures of night. You have no business with the child. Let him be.'

'It is *you* have no business with him,' said the harsh voice. Bertrand peered into the shadows, trying to discern the other's features more clearly. Neither he nor his deformed companion could be properly seen. This was not just a product of the darkness of night, Bertrand knew. It was part of the spell such creatures cast, mazing the eyes and perceptions of humans. But he was puzzled. The creatures had indeed stopped, as korrigans were bound to do, faced not only with cold iron but a prayer and a charm.

Yet they seemed not to be frozen, or held, only shifting uneasily beyond the subtle glow of the drawn blade.

As to Alain, he too, had half-vanished in the shift of shadow and light; but Bertrand saw with some fear that the boy seemed to be limply hanging between the two beings. If they had touched him, held him, he might be as good as lost, as so many others had been to *mabrokorr* and its deathly enchantments.

A half-remembered story about something terrible that had happened to the wards of Dame Viviane fleeted for an instant into his mind. They had vanished, never to be seen again. And now Alain was being forced step by step into *mabrokorr*, also to be never seen again . . .

With a muffled roar, he launched himself forward; an action and a cry that was echoed by the young Goddamn. Yet Bertrand still held the sword before him, higher now, trying to illuminate the creatures. If they could only see them, then somehow, his mind wildly ran, they might have a chance at snatching Alain back. He did not wonder at the thought he and the Goddamn were in this together now.

'Move in on the right, I'll take the left,' he shouted. 'Keep moving, say all the prayers you can, and all the charms too!'

The other nodded, and did exactly as he was told. Bertrand, meanwhile, moved ceaselessly in the other direction, holding up the sword, chanting and praying too. Though they could not get any closer to the korrigan-things, it seemed as if all this activity and noise bothered them, for they did not attempt to break out of the circle thus described by the two young men, only moved restlessly back and forth within it, Alain like a limp rag between them.

Now and then, Bertrand caught glimpses of the creatures' forms: he thought that the shorter one must be a *ðuz*, but the other was unlike any korrigan he had heard of, with that hideous face, and twisted, deformed body, looming arms, clawed feet . . . It had a female look to it, too, with long, lank, straw-coloured hair hanging down, and he thought it looked like a harpy, remembering a picture old Sieur Gwazig had shown him once, in a book of the Gospels; a hideous bird-woman with vicious heart and terrible eyes, a tearing beak and sharp claws to rip sinners' flesh. It had horrified him then; it horrified him now. But he was not one to give up. And neither was the Goddamn, by the look of him. His stubbly jaw was set firm; his bright dark eyes flashed, and the handsome face that was built to be merry, under the thatch of floppy fair hair, was full of an iron-hard determination. Faster and faster they circled, louder and louder they chanted and prayed. The things seemed trapped within the circle, but still they could get no closer. Then, all at once, the harsh voice called out, 'Rouanez! Rouanez! Come to our aid, or else all is lost! All is lost!'

They are tiring, thought Bertrand, with a surge of triumph; 'Let us press harder, harder! Faster! Faster!' he yelled to the Goddamn, who nodded, and shouted out words Bertrand had no idea of, on and on and on, gibberish, it appeared. Words were pouring out of his own mouth too, gibberish he knew, yet with a strange power, driven by something whispering in his heart: and then their feet moved, one step forward, and another, and another. 'Rouanez!' chanted the harsh voice, with a hallucinatory, insistent rise and fall. 'Rouanez! Great Rouanez, send us help! Send us help!' Another step ... another ... and then something vast and white and whirling swooped down upon them, something choking and suffocating, catching them by the throat, blinding them, spinning them round, disorienting them, a roaring and shrieking filling their ears, thumping in their blood, pounding in their heads, drawing them relentlessly into madness and terror. 'Come no closer! Retreat! Retreat!' came the other voice they'd heard earlier, the sweet, light one, filled now with a desperate urgency. 'Retreat, retreat, or you are doomed! Doomed!'

Bertrand never knew how long it was he and the Goddamn were trapped in the enchanted mist; nor did he know how they managed to pull their way out of it, only that something was pulling at him, dragging him away, and that as the roaring and shrieking grew less, the suffocating terror was ebbing, he heard the sweet light voice whispering, 'Find Dame Viviane ... find Dame Viviane ... and Estik ... oh find them—' And the sorrow in that whisper was such that he thought he might weep forever from the pain of it; he could not reply. Then, with a wrenching suddenness, the white fog vanished, pulling away from him like skin peeling, and he found himself face down in the dirt, weeping as if his heart was breaking.

He wept for a moment or two, wild fury and unbearable melancholy swelling in him together, pounding in every fibre of his body. Then he realised he was not alone; he sat up and rubbed at his filthy face, pushing at his swollen eyes.

The Goddamn was sitting just opposite him. He too looked a sight: dirt-streaked, hair standing on end, face pale as clay. Yet there was a strange dancing light in his eyes, and a defiant twist to his lips. 'Well,' he said, looking back at Bertrand. 'They are gone.'

'We lost,' said Bertrand, heavily.

The Goddamn shrugged. 'For the moment.'

Bertrand looked away. His heart was too full of sorrow to say anything much. But the Goddamn had no such restraint. He jumped to his feet. 'Come on, man.'

Bertrand stared at him dully. The Goddamn frowned. 'Come *on*.'

'You heard it too?' said Bertrand, at last.

The Goddamn nodded. 'Of course. We have to find Dame Viviane, and Estik, whoever they might be.'

Bertrand hesitated. 'They . . . I think I know Dame Viviane, anyway,' he said with an effort.

'You do?' The Goddamn smiled warmly. He reached down a hand to help Bertrand up. 'All to the better, then.'

'You think . . . you think we should go after them?' Bertrand could hardly recognise himself. What had this done to him? Usually, he would have been racing to go off on adventure, to follow the path, to avenge wrong. This time, a strange heavy hesitation was holding down his limbs; a pain cold as iron had entered his soul.

The Goddamn shook his head, wonderingly. 'Of course we should go. Don't you want to save the boy?'

Bertrand looked away again. Save the boy! Once a person was in the clutches of the korrigans, nothing and no-one could save them.

The Goddamn frowned. 'Very well, then, I'll go on my own, if you will kindly tell in which place I may find Dame Viviane.'

His eyes widened. 'Dame Viviane,' he repeated. 'Isn't she the one Merlin was in love with? Isn't she a powerful enchantress?'

'Wrong one, friend,' said Bertrand, with a dark humour. 'This one is just an old woman. And Merlin vanished centuries ago.'

'Ah well,' said the Goddamn, 'I should have paid more attention to my Da, then, when he told me those stories. Tell me, then, where I may find this old woman?'

Bertrand looked at him. Something in the other young man's face and manner made a little of the darkness lift from his soul for an instant. He said, with a twist of his lips, 'You are the eager one, aren't you? What is your name?'

'I am Walter Owen David Davies of Hereford, at your service,' said the young man, promptly, 'but my friends call me Wat. And you?'

'I am Bertrand du Gwezklen. Stay . . . you are a Goddamn, yet you speak our tongue?'

'A Goddamn?' Wat frowned, then smiled, a darting smile of considerable charm. 'Oh, *God damn*! I see! Yes, I suppose we soldiers curse too much. As to understanding your tongue; it's not so different to Welsh, see, and I know Welsh because Da's Welsh though living in Hereford amongst the er, the Goddamns. Mam was English, though she's passed over now. I'm . . . well, I'm a borderlander, I suppose. Neither one nor the other, but both too, if you take my meaning. I engaged as a soldier with Sir Ralph de Courcy, who is the lord of our manor, and they were glad of me, see, on account of I speak enough to be understood here—'

'I see,' said Bertrand, though he was only dimly sure he did. Yet Wat's flow of words had a calming effect on him; the iron sorrow that had bitten into his soul didn't seem quite as painful now.

'See, Bertrand,' said Wat, eagerly, watching his face, 'it would be better if you and I went looking for this old lady and the other one, given as you know the country and I don't.'

Bertrand studied him. 'You would be deserting,' he observed, quietly.

Wat shrugged. 'Bah! That happens all the time. You must know that. Doesn't it happen here?'

'All the time,' said Bertrand, sighing, 'and it's not so hard to know why.'

'I hate all this looting and pillaging and things we have to do to survive,' Wat said. 'It wasn't why I took up the sword! We were told it was for honour; well, I have to say it was for adventure too. But there's been precious little of both. Sir Ralph was a good man, but he was killed almost as soon as we set foot in this country, and his son is a fool and a brute. I do not wish to serve under him. I was planning to leave soon anyway. So why not now? And why not on a real task? You should come with me.'

Bertrand hesitated only a fraction more. 'My men—' he began.

'Are long gone,' finished Wat promptly, 'and won't be back, I'll be bound.'

Bertrand sighed. In his bones he felt Wat was right. But what if he were not? 'My fallen men: I should arrange to have them buried.'

'They'll be buried with our dead,' Wat replied. 'We're not heathens or savages, you know.'

'Is that so?' said Bertrand, dryly.

Wat grinned. 'We were told you were!'

Bertrand shrugged. 'They might be right at that,' he said, with a small laugh. 'Well, then, Wat, our way lies to Broceliande. I come from there, and that was the last place I saw Dame Viviane. It may be that someone there may know where she is. As to the other – Estik – that means nightingale. I wonder if—'

'Broceliande!' breathed Wat, interrupting him. 'Why, that's where Merlin—'

'Yes, that's right.' Bertrand brushed himself down, picked up his sword, which had flown out of his hands when the fog had descended, and sheathed it. He looked at Wat. 'Ready, then?'

'Ready!' echoed Wat, falling into step beside Bertrand. 'Did you hear what that dwarf thing called out, before the fog came down on us?'

'He called on Rouanez,' said Bertrand, shortly. 'His Queen. Queen of the korrigans, the fairies.'

Wat nodded, slowly, his eyes shining. 'She must be a powerful one,' he observed.

'They usually are,' sniffed Bertrand, and strode off down the path, Wat hurrying after him.

Thirteen

'I heard you, I heard you, Ragnell-girl,' said the *duz*, a malicious whine in his voice. 'I will tell Rouanez what you said, how you told them to find the Viviane and the Estik.'

Tiphaine stopped in her headlong rush. She stopped so abruptly that Gwengan almost fell over, and the boy whose arm she was supporting swayed in her grasp. 'If you breathe one word, Gwengan,' she hissed, 'if you even so much as think about it, I will tell Rouanez what is in your heart. I will tell her of your greed for gold, and how you are prepared to stop at nothing to get it.' She held the *duz*'s cold-burning eyes with a glare of her own; and after an instant, the creature dropped his gaze. 'Do you understand, Gwengan?'

The *duz* shivered. Tiphaine could almost have pitied him; but she hardened her heart to it. This was a battle she did not intend to lose. An iron had entered her soul; a determination not only to survive, but to triumph over the korrigans. 'Well, Gwengan?'

'I understand,' said the *duz*, dully. 'I will say nothing.'

'And we are not taking this child to Rouanez,' Tiphaine went on. At these words, the *duz*'s head snapped up, his eyes wide. 'No,' went on Tiphaine, 'I will not take another child to be imprisoned in *mabrokorr*.'

'But . . . but you heard her—' Gwengan's voice was shaking. 'If you do not bring him to her, you will never see your brother again, and you will be condemned always to live in that bird-form.'

'I will not bring the child to Rouanez,' repeated Tiphaine, as if the *duz* had not spoken. 'I will bring Rouanez to him instead. And then we will see what we will see.'

The *duz* shivered again. 'We will be stone pillars, or ants, or leaf-mould,' he moaned. 'She will never forgive you, or me, what is more. You cannot summon a Queen of the korrigans just like that, at your pleasure, Ragnell-girl!'

'Oh yes, I can,' said Tiphaine, with more conviction than she felt. 'I will make it worth her while.' She spoke calmly, but inside her, a terror greater than any she had ever known hollowed out her belly. Was she completely mad? How did she think she was going to win against the Queen of the korrigans? What had possessed her to think she could? Oh, but she knew the answer to the last question: it had been the sight of Alain's white face, his fear when he saw her and Gwengan. She could not do it, then; she could not deliver up a child in ransom for her own life and that of her brother's. She had to find another way. Or several ways, to be precise, combined. One was keeping out of *mabrokorr*, where Rouanez's powers were limitless, dodging her in *mabroden*, where she could only interfere at certain times and places. Of course, Rouanez still had powers even now: witness her sending of the magic fog to disorient the young men. But she could not manifest, except with difficulty, in *mabroden* right now.

Another aspect was truth-telling, or rather, the avoidance of it. Korrigans hated lies; it was what they most hated about humans. They themselves could not tell lies: or at least, could not if they were challenged to tell the truth. They were bound to tell truth; only korrigans contaminated by enslavement in the human world, or voluntary exile in it, would break that bind. And in this maybe lay the beginning of an answer. In *mabroden*, Tiphaine's *daouden*, her inner self, would be only a mist to the korrigan Queen; it was only in the korrigans' country that it could be seen clearly. And so she would not be able to see what Tiphaine chose to keep hidden. Mind you, the korrigans had ways of forcing such things into the open, if they suspected duplicity; and if Rouanez chose to mobilise all her resources against Tiphaine, then —

But she would not think about it. She would not defy the Queen directly; she would find some plausible reason why Alain could not be taken right now to *mabrokorr*; she would lure the Queen into her net. And for that, she had to have Gwengan sufficiently cowed and pliable as well.

She looked at the *duz*, and let her lips curve into a cruel grimace. 'You had best do as I say, Gwengan. Or else —' The *duz*'s eyes went dead. He hunched his shoulders. He knew power when he saw it. And it was his reaction more than anything else that made Tiphaine realise that she did have some kind of power: though what it was, she was not sure yet. It could not just be the power of extreme loathliness: the *duz* would hardly care about that. It must be more than the power of menace, conveyed convincingly, for if Rouanez did know what was in the *duz*'s heart, she would have punished him as being potentially treacherous. No; it must be because the *duz* had been a slave before, to a powerful man, and that in Tiphaine, he had recognised something similar to that man. Tiphaine did not want to think about that either, and what it meant. To her younger, more innocent self, it would have been a matter of horror. Now it felt like something ugly and painful, but necessary. Just as she had to tell lies, so Gwengan had to be her slave until such time as it was no longer necessary; she could not trust him in any way.

'I understand,' said Gwengan, softly. The deadness in his eyes went beyond mere despair.

'Very well,' said Tiphaine, coldly. 'If you do as I say, all will be well. When all is done, I will obtain for you your heart's desire, and you can then choose what you want to do. But until then, I bind you to me with links of power that cannot be broken, Gwengan.' And she laid a hand on his head and whispered some words; words of ritualistic strength which would hold the *duz* more tightly indeed than chains of iron. As she did so, she felt a coldness entering into her through the hand that rested on the *duz*'s rough head. The terror churned in her then; for she knew without having to be told what the coldness meant. It was korrigan coldness. The touch of korrigan blood the Queen had sensed in her; she was inviting it into her being, it was no longer pushed under by her *daouden* but brought out into the upper levels of her heart and mind. She had changed in *mabrokorr*: changed forever, within as much as without. How long would it be, her *daouden* whispered faintly to her, how long would it be before inner loathsomeness matched outer? For with these words, you have put *me* behind bands of steel; words of iron. You have hidden me from Rouanez's sight, but will you ever find me again? You are turning into a korrigan, my Tiphaine, and I will never be with you again . . .

Oh, but I must do this, I must, she answered, desperately; I must, to save Alain and Gromer too. There is no other way. And you, my *daouden*, you must stay hidden, I must hide you from her, for both our sakes, and the sake of this child, and my brother —

The *daouden* did not answer, for it had retreated behind the cold wall. Tiphaine felt its absence like a darkness in her being, and she had no way of knowing if that darkness would ever lift. But she had no choice. By tricking Rouanez, enslaving Gwengan, and making her own *daouden* retreat, she might find the strength to defeat the denizens of *mabrokorr*, without endangering either the child or her brother. With a little luck, those two men would find Dame Viviane and Estik, though that was a wild card rather than a certainty, and she had no idea if it would work, if they would believe her or want to act on it. Yet the thing she had glimpsed in the plain young man's eyes – horror and fear mixed with sorrow – made her hope they might do so. She could not rely on it; she must primarily rely on herself, and the cunning she had learnt in *mabrokorr*. That cunning told her Rouanez would never form an alliance with Bubo against Tiphaine if she thought her advantage still lay against him. Gromer would be safe so long as the two korrigans were enemies or rivals.

And so she would have to contact Bubo too, and try and make him believe in his own advantage.

She looked at the ∂uz. 'First things first,' she said, briskly. 'The boy must be made safe from Rouanez's spies.' The ∂uz's eyes flicked to the boy, swaying unsteadily, eyes closed, on Tiphaine's arm, but he said nothing. 'As must we,' she added, with a small laugh. 'We will send word of our intentions to Rouanez. Then we will travel to Archduke Bubo's country.'

Gwengan's eyes widened, but all he said was, 'Very well, mistress. I am eternally at your service.'

'Call on the Queen, Gwengan,' said Tiphaine. She knew it had to be here, in Stone Wood, where Rouanez could not break through in her own form.

The ∂uz's hair stood straight on end, his teeth chattered, his skin went a strange shade of clay-grey. But he closed his eyes, muttered, 'Very well, mistress,' and he began to chant as he had done earlier. 'Rouanez! Great Rouanez! We crave word! We crave word!'

Silence. The ∂uz's eyes opened in fright. He stared at Tiphaine. 'She knows, Ragnell-girl,' he whispered, brokenly. 'She will punish us—'

'Nonsense,' said Tiphaine, robustly, though her knees shook. There was something sinister about that silence: something watchful, and yes, knowing. 'Do it again,' she snapped. 'She may not have heard you.'

The ∂uz gave a harsh laugh. But he began chanting again, obediently, 'Great Rouanez! Rouanez! We crave—'

'I heard you the first time,' burst a voice in on the air, so suddenly that neither Tiphaine nor Gwengan could quite repress a little gasp. 'Such impatience, Gwengan, when I am busy. Now, what word is this you crave?'

The Queen's voice was not angry, not menacing, only touched with that petulant impatience so characteristic of korrigans. Tiphaine took heart at that. She thought, she may be able to see us, right now, but she cannot see inside me. She cannot see my *daouden* at all. She put on a humble, beseeching voice.

'Your Majesty, it is I, Ragnell-girl, who asked Gwengan to send you word. There is something I must tell you.'

'Indeed?' said the Queen, and into her voice had immediately leapt a sharpness, a suspicion. Tiphaine's skin crawled. The lie she was about to utter chilled her blood. She whispered, 'My lady, the boy you wanted: there is something wrong with him.'

'Wrong with him? Whatever do you mean? I think I can be the judge of that,' said Rouanez, and now the suspicion was sharper in her voice, and Tiphaine could feel the cold, clear glass of her mind groping for Tiphaine's, trying to probe, to see, to know. Tiphaine held herself as stiffly as she could.

'I think it may be difficult for you, my lady,' she replied, firmly. 'You see, it is that his *daouden* has been taken from him.'

A small silence, then Rouanez burst out with, 'What! How can that be!'

Tiphaine shook her head. 'It is so, lady. I can feel it. His *daouden*: it is not there. It has been taken from him.'

'He doesn't have one, then,' said Rouanez, after another silence. 'It is as I said: he is a korrigan, stolen from our world into theirs.'

Tiphaine's forehead broke out into a cold sweat. This

was the most dangerous part. 'No, your Majesty,' she said, quietly. 'He is not a korrigan, not a changeling child. He is a human one, but he has been most grievously changed. His *daouden* – it was taken from him by korrigans . . . By none other than Archduke Bubo himself.'

Rouanez's roar filled the forest. Gwengan shook with fear. Alain stayed insensible, but his whole body shivered. Tiphaine kept a tight grip on him.

'Bubo! Bubo! Why would Bubo do such a thing! How dare he!' Rouanez's voice shook with fury, and an odd kind of anxiety. Tiphaine thought, she's biting, she's biting, she is suddenly back in the full of her rivalry with Bubo, she thinks he's gaining on her, she thinks he's cheating, too. An unholy joy, a cold exaltation filled her.

'Your Majesty,' said Tiphaine, 'I could scarcely believe it myself. But the boy himself told me, before . . . before you saved us from the two interfering humans. He said that it was by way of being a threat, a ransom: the boy would never get his *daouden* back if the boy himself did not go to live in Bubo's court, and make music for him there, the sweetest music that ever was, as — '

'I know, I heard it,' growled Rouanez. 'That explains why the music was so like the most beautiful of *mabrokorr* songs. But it is wrong. He cannot do this. He cannot! He must be stopped! He is getting well above himself!' The anxiety had given way to a cold anger. The korrigan Queen was well and truly hooked. Her next words showed it clearly.

'Ragnell-girl, I want you and the *duz* to travel at once to the Archduke's court and demand the meaning of this foolishness. Remind him of our pact. Remind him that he cannot simply do as he pleases, like . . . like a human!' Her voice stung like a whip.

Tiphaine bent her head humbly. 'Your Majesty, I stand ready to do whatever you want.'

'You are to take the child with you. We will need to keep him safe until he can be reunited with his *ðaouðen*. And to do so, it will be necessary to change his shape.'

'Why . . . I don't understand . . .'

'You don't need to,' snapped Rouanez. 'Listen carefully. In Stone Wood grows a little flower we call *neuið*. The *ðuz* will show you where to find it. Pick one petal – and one petal only – of the *neuið*, and put it under the child's tongue. It will do the rest. Do you understand, Ragnell-girl?'

'Yes, your Majesty.'

'The *neuið* charm will only last a short while, though; enough to get you to Bubo's lands, but within the day, it will fade, and he will be revealed for who he is. So take care.' Rouanez' voice went very quiet. 'But remember, Ragnell-girl; if you should think to trick me, or bluff me, or deceive me in any way, and I find out, then my vengeance will be terrible. I lay this binding on you: that you cannot regain the love of your brother, or your true shape until you come back to *mabrokorr*, bringing the child with you. Unless—' Her voice trailed away.

'Unless—' whispered Tiphaine, but Rouanez snapped, 'That is for you to find out if you can. I will never tell you, and nor will any korrigan. But if you keep to your side of the bargain, I will deal fairly with you. Now – to get you to Bubo's court. You will have to travel fast, for it lies many leagues distant from here, a long way in the forest the humans call Broceliande. There is a white oak tree there – Dergwenn – which is the portal to Bubo's lands. You will have to give a password to be allowed through. This password is *Luchatenvelded*.'

'*Luchatenvelded*,' repeated Tiphaine, frowning a little; it seemed like a nonsense word, and yet it reminded her of something . . . But before she could think what it was, Rouanez's voice broke into her thoughts, sharply.

'You must remember it, and not be diverted into thinking it is not right. Once you have passed through the door and into Bubo's dukedom, you will also need to remember that though it is *mabrokorr*, like here, it is not quite the same kind as here. It is a different country, though in the same world. Keep your eyes and ears open, and your wits about you. And one more thing. Do not, under any circumstances, tell your brother who you really are, if you want to get out of there, regain him, and your own true shape.'

Tiphaine's heart thumped. 'I will remember,' she said. 'I thank you, your Majesty.'

'Bah,' said Rouanez, with a harsh laugh, 'keep your thanks for later. Go. And take care not to forget what I have told you.'

'I will,' murmured Tiphaine, but Rouanez did not answer. She had gone. Tiphaine stood for an instant, Alain's body warm against her, gently warming her chilled being, and she thought: Yes, it is done; we have a chance now; she fell for it. And yet a tiny part of her was dismayed by how easily the whimsical korrigan Queen had been persuaded; how easily she herself, as a prize, had been pushed aside in favour of the shiny new toy, Alain, and the rivalry with Bubo. More, something felt withered and wrong in her. She remembered her *ðaouden*'s words, about taking care that inner loathsomeness did not match outward ugliness, and her whole being trembled. But it was too late now for regret. She had to be strong. She could not trust Rouanez's promises, of course; but at least she had a chance now.

She looked down at Gwengan. 'So, *ðuz*. We go. You heard the Queen. We have to find this *neuið*.'

'Very well, mistress,' said the *ðuz*, obediently.

Fourteen

*I*n the last five years, Dame Viviane and Estik
had wandered the whole length and breadth of
Brittany and beyond. They had crossed the Loire and
gone down into the lands beyond, into the waterlands
of Aquitaine. In each place they went, they tried to find
news of the korrigans who had taken the children away.
But not a whisper did they hear, only great growlings
of war in the human world, and turmoil, and families
uprooted everywhere, so that none seemed to care
about the disappearance of just two children.

And then one day they came to a place that lay
between the ocean and the river, a river so large here
that it resembled rather a lake. There, at lands-end, on
a silver spit of beach between the two waters, they
came across an old hermit, fossicking for shellfish at
the edge of the tide. His name was Blamor, and he
said he was a great-great-great-great-great cousin of
Lancelot of the Lake, who had come from that place.
Because Viviane and Estik were hungry and thirsty,
and because he was lonely, Blamor took them to his
hut in the reeds, which was all, he said, that remained

126

of the buildings of Lancelot's time. He talked a great deal about these old times, almost as if he had been there, and Viviane listened, without asking him the question she had asked everyone else about Tiphaine and Gromer.

Now Viviane knew that those who shared Lancelot's blood were often reputed to have second sight. But she also knew they had the reputation of not liking to share that gift with just anybody. So she did not ask Blamor immediately for news of Tiphaine and Gromer.

Instead, she brought the conversation around, gently, letting Blamor know she herself was a Guardian, that Estik was her companion. Therefore, the old man would know they themselves were of double vision and to be trusted.

But still she breathed no word of her quest, though she felt for the first time in a long time that there was modest hope. In this strange, timeless, in-between place between water and land, away from the clamour of battle, listening to the old man recount adventures and strange happenings from the distant past, she and Estik for the first time felt a measure of rest and peace. They stayed longer than they meant to, on account of this; and on account of the fact that Viviane still felt reluctant to ask the question.

But then one misty morning, when the fog shrouded even the water, she and Blamor went for their customary walk on the beach. All at once, Blamor stopped. Facing the direction of the sea, he began to chant. And as he did so, it seemed to Viviane that she could see the place as it had been in Lancelot's day. A great silver-turreted castle rose in the space between land and water. Now she could see a procession approaching the castle, at its head a bareheaded man whose hair gleamed with blue-black light. Next to him was a woman, whose golden hair gleamed not like stray shafts of sun through cloud, but like the hot glow of the slow-descending star. Their faces were turned away from her; but as they passed, very close by, they turned: and Viviane gave a cry of horror, for the face under the woman's blazing hair was hideously ugly, withered and deformed; and that under the man's blue-black glory was one that seemed made of stone: a cruel statue, with lips drawn back in a snarl of vicious violence. And now she saw that behind them was an army of capering, coarse, distorted figures, with cold glares and hard faces.

Cold horror gripped at her but hot tears sprang to her eyes, for despite the cruel distortions, she had recognised the faces of the procession's two leaders. And so the question that had been hovering inside her burst out without thought or planning, 'Oh, Tiphaine and Gromer, where are you? Where are you, that I may save you?'

No answer; but as she watched, behind the procession crept three figures: two young men and a strange creature, with the head of a lizard and the body of a child. And in the creature's hand was a silver harp. Her breath caught in her throat, for the golden-haired horror that had been Tiphaine turned, and silently pointed to the three figures behind her. And then an unfamiliar voice came out of the mist, wafting gently, 'Five years were they taken, and nearly, that is over. Five years are past, and if the song is found, then they might—' The voice died away into silence, though Viviane strained her ears to hear more.

'Oh tell me,' she burst out desperately, 'tell me more, that I—' And she tried to touch the phantoms before her: but as she did, they faded and dissolved into the mists as the voice had done.

Silence; then Blamor's voice called unsteadily out of the fog. 'Dame Viviane, Dame Viviane!' He loomed up beside them, grey-faced. 'Forgive me, I could not hold—'

'I ask you, tell me, if you know anything, if you have heard anything, about my lost children. Why do I see them here? Who were those with them? Are they kept here, in the Lake? And what of the five years? Are they to be released?'

Blamor shook his head. 'I do not know. Have never seen any of them here before.'

'But the castle: it was Joyous Gard—'

Blamor shook his head again. 'I have never seen that castle before either. It is not Joyous Gard. It looks like—' his eyes slid sideways—' a castle in the other place. In the hollow lands.'

Viviane's shoulder ached from Estik's grip; it was probably bleeding, she thought. She could feel something else in the little bird's frail warm body: the tiny vibrations of suppressed song. Estik had the beginnings of hope deep in his being now; and that alone gave her new courage. She touched him once more, then turned to Blamor. She did not ask him to explain the phrase 'other place, the hollow lands', for she knew that was code for the Otherworld. Instead, she asked, 'Where is it, then?'

'I do not know. But the Lake . . . the Lake . . . they might—'

Viviane stood up. She touched Blamor lightly on the

shoulder. 'Please, my dear friend.' That was all she said; but Blamor's eyes filled with tears.

'My . . . Lancelot, he was taken too . . . they meant well by him, and by his cousins . . . but they changed them forever, especially Lancelot, who was there so long. He could never again be the child running on the beach, living in the bosom of his family. They took him from the human world because they had a great fate ready for him, one that would make him live forever in the eyes of men, and the other place too. He was given great gifts, especially that of grace, and love . . . but—'

'But he was forever changed,' said Viviane, softly. 'They took from him something precious, which he would never find again. His memories of childhood would be of the Lake, and not of his own home.'

'Yes,' whispered Blamor. Then he looked straight at Viviane and said, 'Were they the children you were meant to guard? Is this why you wander the earth far from your home, because you did not save them from the fate decreed for them? You, and the nightingale, both?'

Something moved in Estik's throat; a ripple of muscle, a note striving to escape. But the bird stayed mute, and Viviane said, harshly, 'That is so.'

'Ah.' Blamor looked down at the wet sand. His face worked a little, then he said, softly, 'The Lake will help you.' Without another word, he walked deeper into the mist, and Viviane followed, Estik on her shoulder. Louder and louder came the sound of the water, and in a very short time, Viviane felt ripples and waves lapping at her ankles. She could hardly see Blamor in the mist, which seemed to have become both thicker and somehow more translucent.

Blamor began to sing. Softly at first, then louder and louder. Viviane could not understand the words; they seemed to be in a dialect foreign to her, perhaps the ancient language of that place, perhaps something else, pertaining to the Otherworld of the Lake itself. But the song filled her both with a thrilling delight and a feeling akin to an almost unbearable terror. On her shoulder, she could feel Estik shuddering violently, and she put up a hand to calm him. As she did so, the song died away; and in answer came another, floating through the shining mist. A song of immense power and melancholy, deep and wild and yearning, a song, and a presence, that seemed to fill not only the beach, the mist, but every part of the living creatures who stood there waiting. Estik was bolt upright, his claws again digging painfully into Viviane's flesh; but she did not feel it any more. Her eyes were fixed on the glowing, shining mist.

The song ended. Blamor spoke: again in the same foreign tongue. An answering whisper came through the mist. A whisper so soft that Viviane might have thought, the instant after she heard it, that she'd imagined it, if it had not been for Blamor's listening stance. He spoke again; and the voice replied. Then, all at once, the mist parted, and Viviane and Estik saw . . .

Two young men, seated by a fire. Darkness ringed the fire's brave light; but from the thicker shadows in some parts, Viviane could see the two men were in a forest. One of them had a plain, even ugly, honest face, in which shone eyes of great intelligence and sadness; the other had bright, merry

131

eyes under a shock of fair hair. The fair-haired one appeared
to be talking, but the other, though listening, was also
watchful. He kept glancing around him, looking beyond the
ring of fire, as if he could pierce the darkness.

Viviane gasped. She recognised his face, though not
that of the other. Bertrand. Bertrand du Gwezklen,
whom she'd met in the forest of Broceliande maybe the
very day her children had been taken. The thought
made a great bitterness spurt in her heart. Why was
this being shown to her?

Suddenly, a voice spoke inside her head. 'Find them,'
it said. 'Find them – find the one they look for, too –
and you will find what you are looking for. Five years
have passed; and the song is nearly done.'

'But where . . . who—' Viviane said, desperately,
aloud.

'Find them,' the voice repeated. 'Find them—'

'But please . . . you must tell me . . . more—'

But the voice was utterly silent. And Viviane could
feel that the presence had left the beach, where now
reigned a silence composed only of mist and water and
shrouded land. She turned to Blamor. 'Ask . . . please
. . . ask again.' But he shook his head. 'I cannot.'

Blamor's expression forbade her to say more. You
could not force the Otherworld to help you; she knew
too that already she had been told more than perhaps
anyone other than Blamor. She swallowed.

'We will have to go back to Brittany, Estik,' she
murmured. 'Back to Broceliande, to find Bertrand du
Gwezklen, if he's still there—'

Estik shifted uneasily on her shoulder. What if
the boy was not there? How could finding him

help, anyhow? But he was even less eager to question Otherworldly clues than she was. And so he cheeped, gently, to show her he agreed, and would be with her every step of the way.

Fifteen

Wat and Bertrand had journeyed for two days and two nights, keeping to dark paths and tortuous ways, the better to dodge unwelcome curiosity and attention. In general, this was not difficult to evade; there was not much curiosity left in most villagers after years of war. Lone army stragglers like themselves could be dodged; and the predatory gangs of demobbed soldiers who roamed the countryside usually left them well alone, after one look at Bertrand's bulldog fierceness and Wat's wiry strength.

As to the authorities, they were of no concern whatever to the two young men as they made their way to Broceliande, for they did not exist as such. Some summary justice was occasionally meted out to unlucky or stupidly unwary deserters and pillagers if they were ever caught; but as lords and town authorities did not like to pay soldiers, even desertion was not regarded particularly as a crime worth spending time and money on.

As to curiosity of another kind – the attention of the Otherworld – so far they had managed to avoid it.

They had not seen again the hideous creature and the *∂uz* who had taken Alain; and they had not met any other korrigan along the way. Perhaps this was just a false peace, and the korrigans were waiting to ambush them in Broceliande. The answer to that lay in the identity of the one who had begged Bertrand to find Dame Viviane. It could not have been the things that had taken Alain; and it had not sounded like the boy's voice either.

Bertrand pondered and pondered on this problem as he and Wat made their way south and west, and he had come to the conclusion that it had been a woman's voice, a human woman, with a terrible burden of sorrow in it. Perhaps another one taken by the korrigans, who grieved for Alain too? He remembered the horror that had settled on him, the iron despair, and thought, maybe that's what she felt, she whose sorrow filled my heart..But if so, who was she? And might he be able to help her as well as Alain? Sweet and light, yet with that undertone of sorrow, it had been a voice full of beauty, he thought. And in his mind and heart, as he journeyed on, an image had grown, of a lovely girl with the face of an angel and the courage of a lion, a girl whose laughter and ease had been stolen by thoughtlessly cruel and vicious korrigan whim. He did not know it yet, but he was already halfway to falling in love with the girl in this vision.

Of course, he did not speak of this to Wat, except to nod seemingly incuriously at the other man's chatter about who their helper might have been. Wat was nearly driven mad by that incuriosity. He was interested in everything and everybody, and this adventure struck him as a particularly exciting one. He plied Bertrand with questions about the korrigans, trying to determine if they were indeed similar to the Fair Folk, or the Twylyth Teg, as his father would have called them, back home. Bertrand's monosyllabic answers did not discourage him; in his heart and mind was growing a vision of an adventure such as no man he knew had ever experienced. He would match wits with the korrigans, he thought; he would use his knowledge of the Fair Folk to second-guess their Queen. He did not tell Bertrand any of this, for it was still only a vague vision agitating in him. Instead, he chattered brightly about his home, and told stories of his brothers and sisters, and of how his oldest sister had given birth to his first nephew not long before he left. Bertrand listened with half an ear; his own life had been very different to Wat's, and he could hardly put himself in the other man's shoes. Warmth and joy had been the other's experience, of an unquestioned and freely accepted kind; this was not something he'd known, though he'd been happy enough, back home in Broceliande. Happiness – it meant so many different things to so many different people, he thought as they trudged on. For the girl who was prisoner of the korrigans with Alain, what would happiness mean? Some thought the korrigans' world, with its magic and its potential to make every wish come true, its ease and lack of strong emotion, was a dream of true happiness. Some thought happiness lay in money, or power, or in making a loved one one's own, or in so many other things. And there were those, like Wat, who were happy through the sheer joy of being alive. That was a real gift, thought Bertrand, glancing sideways at the irrepressible Goddamn as he told yet another story of home. And an affection grew in him for the other man; an affection all the stronger for being unspoken.

At length, on the morning of the third day, they reached the outskirts of the great forest, and plunged into it. And Bertrand, who had not been back here for five years, found his heart assailed by pain as he saw the changes wrought on the villages of Broceliande. All too many of them had only women and children, old men and young boys living in them: no males between the ages of twelve and fifty. It was not that crops had been untended or that things were in disrepair; people had obviously tried to keep life functioning. But it was difficult, when so many were missing; and as well as weariness, there was a certain resentment in the faces of many of those left behind. They learnt soon enough what that resentment came from, when they stopped to ask in one village yet again – and vainly – about Dame Viviane's whereabouts.

The person they had asked was a tall, strong, athletic-looking woman in her thirties or so, who turned out to be the lady of one of the smaller manors of Broceliande. Her kirtle pinned up, her face brown from being out in the fields with her workers, she was obviously not the kind of lady who had sat back and given orders. She was coarsened from her work, yet there was still an imperiousness in her gaze, an imperiousness born of her own belief in herself and her family.

'Ask rather where my lord is,' she said tartly. She pointed to the groups of women and girls and young boys and old men labouring in the fields, and glared at the two young men. 'Ask where their husbands are, and their sons and older brothers. Ask why they have left so lightly and easily, and what it is they seek so far from their home, which needs them. Ask yourselves, my friends, what it is you do, far from your home!'

'This *is* my home,' said Bertrand, quietly, breaking into her anger. 'Or at least as close to it as makes scarcely a difference. Is Sieur Gwazig still in the forest, lady?'

The woman stared at him. Her eyes, which had sparked into such sudden fury, lost their brilliance. She said, gently, 'Forgive me. I do not know what came over me. In the old days I would never — ' With an effort, she went on, 'Sieur Gwazig is no longer here. Many years ago, he had a summons from the Duke, to see him at court.'

'Ah yes, I remember.'

'He never returned. No-one knows where he is, or even if he is still alive. Certain it is that he is not at the Duke's court. Or here.'

Bertrand said, softly, 'God save him. We live in evil times.'

She sighed. 'We do.' Her hands clenched together. 'And now, I must get back to work.'

Much had changed here. So much. In the old days, she would have asked them their names. She would have made it her business to know why they sought Viviane, would have sent someone to help them find her. Now, she looked dully away from them, obviously hoping they would soon leave. But Bertrand ignored Wat's meaningful gesture to move on, and asked, gently, 'Who is left of the manor of Yann de Broceliande?'

The lady started. She looked properly at Bertrand, trying to place his face. He said, 'I am Bertrand du Gwezklen, lady, and this is my friend, Wat. I lived on the manor of Sir Yann de Broceliande.'

Her face flooded with colour. 'Oh! Sir Yann and his family have left, this many long—'

'I know,' said Bertrand, sadly. 'Sir Yann is dead now. But his daughter and her aloof French husband: they live at the court of the King of France, who has promised to protect them.'

She made a face. 'And they are not coming back. Even though the manor is practically in ruins now, what with the steward drinking himself half to death and everything running riot—'

Bertrand shook his head. 'The Frenchman has rich holdings,' he said, heavily. 'What care does he have for a little manor in Brittany, especially now?'

She looked deep into Bertrand's eyes. 'So you have come back to undo the wrong that was done to that place, Bertrand du Gwezklen.'

His breath caught in his throat. But he replied, steadily enough, 'I have come back to undo wrong, yes.'

Her face changed. She knew he meant not to go back to the manor. She said, 'May God be with you, then.'

It was a dismissal. But Bertrand asked, gently, 'Could you tell me . . . Lady . . . could you tell me if there has been any activity near Dergwenn?'

'Dergwenn!' Her hands clutched at her skirt. 'No. Why? What do we care for *them*, now, that—' She broke off as Bertrand put a finger to his lips. 'Best not to say it out loud, Lady.'

'What would you know?' she flashed out at him, and turned on her heel and walked away.

'Well,' said Wat, staring after her, 'she was a termagant, and no mistake!'

'She had the right to be,' said Bertrand, shortly. He was not feeling at ease with himself or his task any more. Should he, rather than chasing will o'the wisps around the countryside, be returning home to work hard on the reconstruction of the manor? The little holding he'd had there – it had been his only home. Yet it had not been his, something whispered to him, not truly his, for the land had belonged to Yann de Broceliande and his heirs. He was simply free to work it and use it for his ends. But it did not belong to him. Yet did he belong to it? It called him even now. Should he not be . . . But even as his home called him, the task that had been laid on him was proving too strong. He could, he would return home, just as soon as he had freed Alain, and the mysterious girl, from the clutches of the korrigans. And to get to them, he'd have to brave the one place that he'd avoided all his life . . .

'Wat,' he said, turning to his friend. 'We have to find Dergwenn.' It was said matter-of-factly, as if his breath wasn't catching in his throat at the thought, and his palms prickling with sweat. All the stories he'd ever heard about the strangeness of Dergwenn were filling his head, buzzing in his heart. Wat looked at him shrewdly, and simply nodded.

'Well, we'd best do that, then,' he agreed.

Sixteen

iphaine and Gwengan found the *neuid* flower easily enough, though on her own Tiphaine could have looked for it for ever and not seen it. But the sharp eyes and nose of the *duz* had sniffed out the flower almost immediately, growing in the shadow of an elder tree. It was a tiny, unshowy thing: just four green leaves surrounding a fragile, primrose-coloured five-pointed star of a bloom. Gwengan did not seem to like it; he would not go near it, and showed it to Tiphaine by pointing. She bent down to pluck it, and at once realised why Gwengan was frightened of it. For as soon as she touched the plant, it gave an unearthly yowl, a terrifying sound that cut through Tiphaine's bones like an ice dagger. The shock made her snap the stem, instead of just taking one petal, as Rouanez had instructed; and as she grasped it, the stem writhed and hissed in her hand like an angry snake.

'You fool! You fool!' shouted Gwengan. 'It will be no good now!'

Tiphaine gave him a black look. 'You could have warned me.'

The *ðuz* shrugged. His eyes sparkled maliciously. 'You didn't ask.'

Tiphaine stared at him and knew he hated her, and would try and best her at every opportunity. She said, coldly, 'You are bound, Gwengan. You are bound to help me. Tell me what I should do next.'

'Put it under the creature's tongue,' said the *ðuz*, sulkily.

'What, all of it?'

'You've got all of it, you'll have to use it all, before it dies.' And indeed, the plant had gone quiet and limp in her hand. But it was fading; fading fast, getting withered and dusty to the touch in a matter of seconds.

Racing back to Alain's side, she put a hand under his head, opened his mouth with the other hand, and gently inserted the plant under the unconscious boy's tongue. His body gave a jerk; at once, his pale skin began to change colour, his face narrowing, body shortening, lengthening, limbs shrinking, everything getting smaller, smaller. And suddenly, there, cupped in Tiphaine's palm was a lizard, a tiny, graceful thing for all the world like a living jewel.

A silence: then Gwengan burst out laughing. 'Ah, that's a good one! Taking that thing into the Archduke's country! He won't last two minutes there! Ha! He would've been turned into a bird, if you'd done the right thing; but you've misused the *neuið*, and so that's what you get!'

Tiphaine did not answer. She was gently stroking the lizard. 'Don't worry,' she whispered to it, trying to look into its beady little eyes. 'I will protect you. Here, I'll put you in my pocket. You will be safe, I promise you. Don't leave my pocket. Stay there till it is safe.' All these promises, she thought; but can I really protect the poor little thing?

But the lizard must have believed her, for it lay quietly in her pocket then, and later, as they made their way to Broceliande. It rarely came out, and then only to scurry a little on Tiphaine's arm, and into her palm to accept a few insects and grain and flowers she picked for it. Gwengan watched with sardonic amusement. 'Fattening it up for Archduke Bubo's country?' he remarked, once, but got such a glare from Tiphaine that he subsided immediately.

Those few days journeying through the forest roads – for they could not go through towns and villages, looking as they did – seemed to Tiphaine to pass as if in a dream. She hardly noticed the countryside they were passing through; and though her long residence in always-sunny *mabrokorr* had unaccustomed her to the rigours of the Breton climate, she hardly noticed the fact that the weather was getting damper and more uncomfortable. Her mind was almost completely taken up by trying to plan for what might happen once she was in Bubo's territory; but without the help of her *daouden*, it was not an easy task. Her mind was sharp and clear but seemed somehow incapable of putting things together. Gwengan's presence also did not help; she could not help but wonder uneasily whether the binding power she had laid on him was really strong enough or whether the sly creature would find some way of breaking out of it. A *duz* was nothing if not calculating; and a *duz* who had been in contact with humans, even more so. But he seemed to do her bidding willingly enough for the moment, fetching food, watching for intruders and predators, marking out paths. She would just have to keep an eye on him, and never let her guard down.

At last, on the evening of the third day, they came to the outskirts of Broceliande. And here Gwengan displayed a certain kind of nervousness. He kept looking over his shoulder, and starting at shadows, and licking his lips with anxiety every time the wind made the trees move. It was odd, thought Tiphaine; but she did not waste much time thinking about it, for she was glad they had reached this place. Happen what happened; at least here she was closer to Gromer, closer to her aim. Now to get to Dergwenn . . .

'I think it's to the west,' said Gwengan, reluctantly, when she asked him. 'But there's a Guardian there . . . a terrible man . . . he lops off intruders' heads with one stroke of his sword!'

'We have the password,' said Tiphaine, coldly.

'Password!' Gwengan shrugged elaborately. 'Bubo has that changed all the time.'

Tiphaine stared at him. 'We will make them let us through,' she said. 'He will learn we are from Rouanez. Surely he does not dare offend her by lopping off our heads!'

'The Guardian is Bubo's creature, not the Queen's—' said Gwengan sharply. 'You will have to be sure that the password you have is the right one.' His pointed face was alight with malicious curiosity, but Tiphaine said nothing, and just kept walking. *Luchatenvelded*, she murmured to herself, *luchatenvelded* . . . She did not think Rouanez would have given her the wrong password; the korrigan Queen wanted her own way too much. *Luchatenvelded* . . . A korrigan phrase, doubtless, but with that oddly familiar sound . . . The korrigans set a lot of store by the magic of words, and perhaps that was all that was familiar in it: its incantatory sound, its holding of a spell, somehow, within it.

She started. The little lizard that had been the musician Alain was creeping up her sleeve. Scritch, scritch, went the little claws on her flesh. Scritch, scritch. She tried not to shiver as the little creature made its careful, yet darting way up her arm and towards her neck. It reached her left ear, and she felt the scritch, scritch, scritch of its claws again, under the loathsome mixture of feather and scale that covered her neck and head. Then a soft flutter on her ear, an exhalation that was almost like a tiny sigh, and the lizard tucked itself behind her ear. And as it did that, Tiphaine felt a measure of peace come into her being.

Without speaking, she cupped a hand to it, and stroked the little thing, gently. Stay hidden, she told it in her mind, stay hidden, little Skilf, little Claws . . . Stay hidden, for I am afraid of what will happen. And the little lizard – Skilf, as she was now calling him in her mind – moved gently, once more behind her ear, and then was still, as if asleep. Yet still she felt his presence there, and it strangely comforted her.

The wood became thicker and thicker. They were crawling and creeping now, and Gwengan was muttering away to himself in a cross undertone that Tiphaine knew was at least partly composed of fear. At last he said, 'We're very near, Ragnell-girl . . . look —' and he pointed a crooked finger through a thicket.

She looked. The blood was thudding in her head. Were they really here at last? She could see a tree, shining faintly through the thicket; an ordinary white oak, not even particularly big, or tall, but with that faint luminosity to it that in someone unused to the sight of an otherworldly portal, would have made the hair rise on the back of the neck. It did not have that effect on Tiphaine; she was used to the ways of *mabrokorr*, and no longer thought of them as strange or unusual. But behind her ear, she felt the desperate scrabble of little claws, and whispered gently, Do not fear, do not fear, stay still, do not fear.

Turning to Gwengan, she said, briskly, 'Well, come on. What are you waiting for?' She wriggled through the thicket and stood up in the clearing beyond it, scratched and a little bruised, Gwengan following reluctantly in her wake.

She faced the white oak. There was silence all around. Not a soul seemed to stir. No-one appeared to be barring the way to Dergwenn. But Tiphaine knew the korrigan world. Nothing was ever straightforward with them. So she stood straight in front of the portal to Bubo's realm, and called out in a strong voice, 'I come from the land of Queen Rouanez, with an embassy to Archduke Bubo, and crave safe passage into this realm.'

Silence. She repeated the phrase, adding this time at the end the password she had been given, '*Luchatenveldeð*!' As soon as the word left her mouth, a great clashing as if of arms filled the clearing; and all at once, from a corner of the clearing, out of the air itself, it seemed, a giant figure came riding in.

It was a horseman in leather armour, face completely hidden by a strange full helmet, all black and silver, crested with a picture of a gigantic bird like a cross between an eagle and an owl. Long black hair flowed

146

under the helmet, cascading over the armour to the middle of the horseman's back. He was mounted on a huge red-eyed black horse whose trappings were all of silver leather. In one hand, the horseman held a silver banner embroidered with the same crest as on his armour; in the other, he held a giant, sharpened wooden stake.

Though Tiphaine was accustomed to *mabrokorr* ways, she had never seen anything like this creature before. She could not help giving a little squeak of dismay, and taking a step backwards. Gwengan, meanwhile, had fallen flat on his face with fear. But soon she had taken hold of herself, and waited proudly while the black and silver apparition reached her, and moved around her, the horse snorting and panting, the stink rising on it of a strange, ghastly quality, the horseman's eyes, though hidden by the helmet, seeming to burn directly into Tiphaine.

'If you are the Guardian,' she said, at last, 'I demand safe passage, as an envoy of Queen Rouanez, and on account of the fact I have the password. *Luchatenvelded*!' At the instant she said it, she knew why the word had been familiar; it was not one but a combination of three Breton words: light and darkness. Light and darkness . . . the korrigans lived between the two, at the intersection of light and dark —

But there was no time to think about it; for the Guardian suddenly spoke, in a voice that was like the breaking of waves on a beach, or like the roar of a summer storm; a voice that seemed, unaccountably to Tiphaine, not to really belong to him. He lifted his stake.

'You are an intruder.'

'I am not,' said Tiphaine angrily, though she was beginning to shake with uncontrollable fear, and Gwengan appeared to have fainted. 'I am an envoy from Queen Rouanez. It will go ill with you if you hurt me. I give you the password: *luchatenveldeð*!'

'That is not it,' said the Guardian, and his voice changed again, this time becoming light, amused, cruel. 'That is not it, Ragnell-girl. You will have to try harder.'

'But the Queen herself told me—' Tiphaine began, then stopped. It was not that she was surprised the Guardian knew who she was; that was to be expected, when dealing with korrigans. It was that niggling feeling that the giant man was not speaking with his own voice. And if that was so, then it was likely that it was Bubo speaking through him. The Guardian might be nothing more than a wraith, an apparition to frighten off the unwary and easily frightened, and not a natural creature at all. Or else it might be a kind of extension of Bubo's own being, sent out like a bait and a warning. Or it could be a spellbound man—

'Well, Ragnell-girl? I give you fair chance. Two chances, since you have already used one by giving me an old password. Guess the real password, the new one, and I might let you in. But if you don't—' the voice broke off into laughter, chilling, indifferent, laughter that told Tiphaine precisely what mercy she could expect from its owner. Which is to say, precisely none.

The Guardian moved restlessly around her, his long black hair swinging from under the helmet. It shone glossily, strongly, and without knowing quite what she was doing, she reached out, and plucked a strand of hair from that glossy mass as it whipped past her.

And the instant she did so, a knowledge came to her, formed by a thought she hadn't clearly seen till that moment.

'*Deizanoz! Deizanoz*!' she cried. Nightandday, nightandday . . .

'Good try, but still not quite right,' said the Guardian, in a thin trickle of sound now, a wary, malicious whisper that made the blood run cold down Tiphaine's spine. Light and darkness . . . night and day . . . the answer must lie in that knowledge, of what lay between them. In-betweeners, that was the korrigan nature. Midday, midnight, dusk and dawn, pivotal, fleeting moments: those were their times. Maybe the password was one of those . . . But which one? She only had one more chance. Only one more.

The strand of hair she had stolen, without the Guardian's appearing to notice – and more than ever, that made Tiphaine think the creature was either possessed or an unnatural wraith – tingled in her palm, like a little shock of crystal, or silver. A strange sorrow, an odd excitement filled her then: but why, she had no clear idea. She hesitated. Then Rouanez's voice came back to her, clearly, coldly. *Do not be diverted into thinking it's not right*. It was a trick, she thought, a damnable, horrible trick, and the knowledge hardened her still further.

But she had said the password first, and it hadn't been accepted: maybe it had to be presented in another way? In a korrigan way?

She put her head back, and sang a song she had heard in *mabrokorr*, in Rouanez's realm.

'Shadows and reflections, secret are we; the korrigans of Brittany, who call on thee. Between day and night, between light and dark we ride, and know no peace, wherever we are. I call on the Archduke to open his gates; I call on the Guardian to unlock the door, for just as it is not day, and it is not night, so dawn and dusk are the same, and the true word of pass we hold: *Luchatenvelded*!'

And as she spoke, the horse snorted, plunged and reared; and the Guardian lifted his stake high, screaming imprecations.

But behind him, the white oak had split open with a tremendous grind and roar, revealing a doorway within it; and Tiphaine sprinted for it, the breath whistling painfully in her chest. As she did so, she saw, out of the corner of her eye, Gwengan getting to his feet, dodging, running, getting in the way of the horse's flying hooves. For an instant the incredible thought leapt into her that the *duz* was actually trying to distract the Guardian; but in the next moment, Gwengan had reached her, and hung grimly to her ankle. 'You're not leaving me here with him!' he screamed, and so the two of them fell through the doorway together, while the Guardian stood frozen in time and space behind them, his sword still held high. But just as Dergwenn shut behind them, Tiphaine saw, with a sudden, paralysing, terrifying flash of sight, that the creature's helmet had half-fallen off: and that the dark eyes that stared coldly and blankly into hers – the eyes of one who no longer has a *daouden* to anchor him – were those of her lost brother, Gromer.

Part Three

Seventeen

*B*ertrand and Wat crouched down in the thicket, hearts thumping. They looked at each other. Wat shook his head. 'He wasn't with them,' he whispered. Bertrand nodded.

'We'll have to follow them, see what's happened,' Wat went on. Bertrand stared at him. 'Well, you heard the bird-hag. She said the password. We can use it too.'

Bertrand said nothing. Wat did not, in his estimation, really understand what they were up against. He peered cautiously in the direction of the Guardian, who was still patrolling the clearing, restlessly. He had never seen such a big man; but it was true to say that the creature, now his helmet was off, did look like a man, if a spellbound one: there was an unfocussed quality to his eyes, like a sleepwalker's. What really worried Bertrand was not the Guardian; but the other creatures, the bird-hag and the *ðuz*, who had slipped through into Dergwenn. Those were truly dangerous; real korrigan-kind, not just enthralled humans.

What had they done with Alain? They might of course have killed him; but on the whole he thought it

153

was unlikely. What had attracted the korrigans' attention to Alain in the first place was his voice, his ability with music. A dead body cannot give them that. No, somehow they must have hidden him; transformed him, perhaps. Had they left him back where they'd started, then? On the whole, he thought not . . . He was inclined to think that Wat was right. To find Alain, they'd have to go into the Otherworld themselves. But it was not a step he would take with any degree of confidence or pleasure. Unlike that fool of a Wat, whose eyes sparkled with anticipation. Bertrand cursed softly to himself. He could have done without Wat's foolhardiness. On the other hand —

It was Wat's nose for something that had led them to this place. He had noticed a faint luminosity through the trees, some distance off, as they were walking along. He had grasped Bertrand by the wrist. 'The Twylyth Teg,' he'd whispered. 'It's them, I'm sure of it . . . it's often like this, at home, when there's a portal open, somewhere, to the Otherworld —'

It had taken Bertrand a moment to remember that the Twylyth Teg was Wat's name for the korrigans. He had looked at Wat, searched his face; then nodded. 'Let's go, then.'

'Of course,' Wat had said as they hurried along, 'it might have nothing to do with what we're after. But you never know. The Twylyth Teg are a curious lot. And they like to do things by the book, wherever you find them —'

And so it had proven to be. They had watched and listened in silence as Tiphaine spoke to the Guardian, and as the giant man crashed around the clearing. Bertrand had felt Wat tremble, like a startled hare; but his eyes still shone brightly. He himself had felt both a shrinking horror and an odd sorrow at the sight of the bird-hag, her ugly, vicious mien, her unnatural face, her extended claws. Korrigans were rarely so ugly. This must be a particularly wicked one, to be so loathsome. And yet . . . he remembered his initial feeling when he'd first seen the face of the bird-hag: poor, poor thing —

Fancies, all fancies. He rose stiffly to his feet. 'Well, Wat, if we're going to do it, we should do it now. I think he can smell us.'

'Yes,' said Wat, glancing at the giant shadows of the Guardian and his horse. He swallowed a little. 'I will come out first, Bertrand. That way I can cover you.'

'I need no cover,' said Bertrand, coolly. 'Just make sure you've remembered the password.'

'Oh yes,' said Wat, 'I can hardly forget it, what with that strange verse she sang! I don't mind telling you I had shivers all over me, then —'

'Me too,' said Bertrand, shortly. He was thinking of how strange it was that the bird-thing had had the correct password all along, but that the Guardian, or some force beyond him, had wanted to play games with her. Gameplaying was of course a korrigan trait, but they did not usually play tricks with words, especially with each other. Spellwords were usually that, unable to be changed or altered or ignored. It was almost as if the Guardian saw something else there, something it did not have to placate or respect. Ragnell-girl, the voice had called her. Ragnell-girl: a strange name for a korrigan.

He shook off his speculations. The Ragnell thing was only a pawn; he had to get to her lord or lady, or whatever it was that had ordered Alain's capture. The *ðuz* too was unimportant, except insofar as *ðuz* were known to be tricky and deceitful creatures, and must be watched. He grasped the pommel of his sword, took a deep breath, and was about to emerge into the clearing, with Wat behind him, when the Guardian gave a great, raucous cry, and cried out. 'Halt! Who goes there!'

And another figure stepped into the clearing – a bent old woman, with a bird on her shoulder. Bertrand shouted, 'It's Dame Viviane!' and without stopping to think, he raced out after her, Wat at his heels, yelling hoarsely, *'Luchatenveldeð! Luchatenveldeð*!'

The Guardian turned; his blank eyes narrowed. A great roar of laughter filled the clearing. 'How many of you little ones are there?' he cried, and in a rapid gesture, he had bent down and scooped up Dame Viviane with one massive hand; then turning, fast as light, he whirled around on the approaching Bertrand and Wat, 'Back! Back!'

'Ah, that, no!' shouted Bertrand, stung into fury. 'Drop her at once!'

'Luchatenveldeð!' shouted Wat, but the Guardian paid no heed. In his massive grasp, Viviane was not moving; she had her eyes fixed on him, however, and there was a strange happiness in her expression which puzzled Bertrand extremely. He drew his sword. 'Fight, coward korrigan, fight! I challenge you! I bind you! You are the Guardian – on guard, then!'

Wat, catching his drift, danced around, shouting insults. 'Korrigan worm! Laidly fool! Otherworldly yellow-belly!'

The Guardian's blank eyes flashed, but he said

nothing, only turned his horse around, and galloped straight for the white oak. But Bertrand and Wat saw that coming, and each flung himself at the horse, on either side. The Guardian plunged his heels into the horse's sides, making the beast scream and rear, and the young men nearly lost their grip. But then Dame Viviane said three loud words, in an unknown language: three words which instantly gentled the horse. So that as the portal swung open before them, the two young men were clinging desperately to the flanks of the Guardian's mount, and still clinging to it when, seconds later, they were tumbling through, into a strange new world.

But not for long; in the next instant, the Guardian had managed to throw them off, and galloped off into the distance with Viviane and her bird companion still held on the saddle in front of him, leaving Bertrand and Wat to roll over and over on the grass. And over and over and over: they could feel the whole ground under them taking mischievous part in rolling them around so they could not stop. In a very short time, Wat was looking almost as green as the grass; Bertrand felt his stomach heave; his wits bounce in his head.

At length, the ground seemed to tire of the game. They were left in a heap, dazed, sick and furiously angry. Wat was the first to recover. 'They're not going to beat us,' he cried, getting gingerly to his feet, 'are they now, Bertrand?'

'I hope not,' said Bertrand, staggering up in his turn, 'but you never know with korrigans . . .'

He looked around him. It was indeed beautiful here, as he'd been led to expect by every story about korrigan country ever told. They were in what appeared to be a most productive orchard, dotted with trees laden with golden fruit. This was set in a glorious green valley, filled with birdsong; with flowers; under a perfect blue sky. Ahead of them, in the distance, could be seen a castle: a pure white castle with silver turrets glittering in the sun. Gazing on the scene, Bertrand's heart became filled with a desperate yearning, a burning nostalgia and longing, but for what he could not be sure. He could hardly be missing this place, as he had never been here before. He turned to Wat, and saw that the same look was on the other young man's face, except even stronger.

'Oh . . . if only I could—'

'Don't say it,' said Bertrand, fiercely, 'or we are lost. And no, don't do that either,' he went on, as Wat's glance turned hungrily towards one of the laden fruit trees. 'If we drink or eat anything here, we're done for.'

'But I need—'

'I've got some bread left, and some water,' said Bertrand. 'That will have to do, till we can get out of here.'

Wat smiled. 'And how are we going to do that?'

'I don't know,' snapped Bertrand, 'but I know I'm not giving in to this place. It's not a good place for us. But we need to find Alain, and Dame Viviane, and bring them home. Do you understand, Wat?' he asked, as Wat's glance wandered. Wat nodded, in an uninterested sort of fashion. Bertrand sighed.

'Come, then,' he said, sharply, and chivvying Wat in front of him like a shepherd his recalcitrant charge, he trudged out of the orchard, and towards the castle that could be seen glimmering in the distance.

It was easy walking, for the grass was soft and

springy to the feet, the air perfumed and warm; yet it was also the hardest thing he'd ever done in his life, for each step seemed to drag, as he fought against his desperate desire to pluck fruit from the trees and eat them till the juice ran down his chin; as he struggled not to stop, to lose himself in dreamy contemplation, as he strove to ignore the sweet voices whispering all around him, urging him to stop.

It seemed to him that each step brought new visions of beauty and contentment; more visions of fruit-laden trees, soft grass, and then, beautiful girls with bared breasts and open arms, calling to him to stop with them, to wait, to linger . . . He was panting from the effort not to give in, and from the effort of keeping Wat walking, as well. He'd had to grasp the other young man by the arm, with a grip of iron, or else Wat would have escaped. And Wat began to curse him for it, too, calling him every vile insult, every bad name, that had seemingly been ever heard in every corner of the world. Bertrand stopped his ears to it, as he veiled his eyes to the beauty around him: he was not to be bought, to be distracted, to be deflected from his purpose. He had heard enough about korrigans to know that sooner or later they would tire of soft temptation, and drag them both in bodily, by force. Till that happened, he would resist. And even afterwards. If will had to be matched against will, he would show them what a human was capable of.

Eighteen

Viviane lay in the Guardian's strong embrace, her heart racing. Gromer! She was sure he was her lost Gromer! She stole a look at the Guardian's blank, dark face. Her Gromer, a Guardian! Could it really be so? She remembered her unease about him, before she left: sometimes talent showed itself in a person not as a small child, but when they entered adolescence. Talent manifested then was very unpredictable and could often be dangerous, especially if it was forced along too quickly. And she had a terrible feeling that it had been, in Gromer's case. Something had seized up in him. His *daouden* was not to be felt. Yet she would know him anywhere. He was her boy, the boy she'd looked after for so long. And those damned korrigans were not going to trick her again. But where was his sister? Was she held here too? She remembered the vision, on the beach in Aquitania, the long golden hair over the ugly face, and shivered a little. But it was not from fear, only happiness that now she was close to one twin, and maybe soon close to the other.

On her shoulder, Estik clung with all the force of his little being. He had been the least able, the least experienced of the three birds Viviane had set as watches over the twins. He had never thought he could ever come to *mabrokorr*, see it with his own eyes, and survive the experience. Yet he had. In his modest way, he did not realise that he had already accomplished a great deal more than any natural bird had ever done before; more not only than one of his class or importance, but any, of any kind. And so he did not know it was that which gave him protection, above all; that, and Viviane's own strength.

In silence, they galloped through the lovely landscape, towards the silver-turreted castle. Along the way, they met groups of people, who stood by to watch them pass, their faces alight with curiosity and yet a strange indifference. Viviane saw that many of them, at least the tallest, handsomest, most human-looking korrigans wore feather cloaks, each one different, from the quietest, downiest sparrow brown to the cascading splendour of peacocks. She felt Estik's interest in this; and his unease too. The birds' plumage displayed all around them felt to him both familiar and frightening; these were creatures who shared in more than one nature. Of course, it was his first visit to the Otherworld, and it was bound to feel strange to him. But this was not the first time Viviane had set foot in the Otherworld; in her long life, and in her capacity as a Guardian, she had been required to go twice, once to return something that had been stolen from the korrigans by one of her charges, and once to escort a changeling child back, in return for the natural child of another of her charges.

This was the third time, then; but the first in which she had gone into a place which was not the *mabrokorr* beyond Stone Wood. She was in foreign territory here, in more ways than one. This was the most dangerous case of all, for Bubo had acted in a way unusual in *mabrokorr*, and she still did not know what that meant, or how Rouanez would react to an appeal, either. And of course, Viviane did not know about Alain, or indeed of Tiphaine's transformation, for not having seen Tiphaine from the front, not looked into her eyes, she had failed to recognise the girl in the deformed bird-hag who had challenged Dergwenn's Guardian. She was sure that Bertrand and his companion would find their way somehow into *mabrokorr*. The little she had seen of them had convinced her they were both brave and resourceful. She did not yet know how the two young men might help in her quest to rescue Tiphaine and Gromer from the clutches of the korrigans, of course, but the vision she had had at the Lake was still strong in her mind, and she was puzzling over its meaning.

They reached the castle, and the Guardian, who was also Gromer, stopped, and dismounted. 'You are to wait here,' he said in a metallic monotone, and strode off, leaving Viviane staring after him with longing and hope. She knew that she must, for the moment, do as she was told; she was well-instructed in the ways of *mabrokorr*. Though that might not necessarily help, if all portents were to be believed; if the Archduke delighted only in breaking rules, not going by them. She was used to the ways of those like Rouanez, who worked to traditional patterns, like korrigans always had. But Bubo had already broken rules: by stealing Gromer from the land bordering Rouanez's country, not his; by making him into a Guardian when he was not ready; by playing tricks with a time-hallowed password into his own country. The thought made her frown a little. She wished she knew more about this place, and its ruler. But just as no-one could know all the countries and principalities and dukedoms and kingdoms of the human world, so one could not know each and every little realm of *mabrokorr*, which was a world as big and diverse as the human world. She knew Broceliande, she had heard of Dergwenn, vaguely; but as her own duties and responsibilities had lain not there but in Stone Wood, she had paid no attention to it. Now she wished she had found out more, but it was too late. She would have to glean facts from what she could, merely by being there.

She was plucked from her thoughts by a hand pulling at her sleeve. Or rather, a claw; for when she turned to see who was trying to attract her attention, she saw a strange, twisted, deformed creature, a thing that looked a little like a cross between a tortoise and a vulture and a sea-thing, with a humped shell-like back, a sharp beak, clawed flippers for arms and yet two legs. It was a thing out of wild dream or nightmare, a thing that for someone of even slightly less than Viviane's strength of mind, would have caused utter horror and fear. But Viviane knew surface appearances were not to be trusted; she had felt the gentleness of the clawed flipper plucking at her; and she saw that the creature's grey eyes were full of suffering, and a great pity stirred in her.

She touched the creature's flippers and said, quietly, 'Who are you, friend?'

The creature ducked its head, and said, quietly, 'My name was Gwazig, in the human world . . . For a long time, I lived in Broceliande . . . until the day when the summons came—'

'Gwazig!' Viviane exclaimed. She had not met the hermit, but had heard of him, of course: his fame as Bonemender had ensured that. 'But how—'

'I received a summons from the Archduke, and had perforce to obey,' said the thing that had been Gwazig, and what might have been a strange little smile briefly highlighted his hideous features. On Viviane's shoulder, Estik shook himself, convulsively.

Viviane reached up to calm him, stroking his soft warm body gently as she replied to Gwazig. 'I do not understand . . . A summons? From the Archduke? But who—'

'The Archduke Bubo,' said Gwazig, with a sigh. 'The ruler of this land. I am bound to him.'

Viviane's eyes narrowed. 'Are you one of the Archduke's kind?'

Gwazig's eyes filled with something indescribable. 'You might say that. I cannot hope that you will forgive me, Dame Viviane.'

'Forgive you?' A beat of premonition ached in her. 'But why?'

He gave a very sad smile. 'I . . . I am not guiltless when it comes to . . . to the children being taken.' She stepped back from him, her hand to her throat, her eyes wide with horror.

'Please understand. I did not take them. But I . . . I am not guiltless altogether. You see, I am the Archduke's brother.'

'His brother!'

'Yes, I was once a great lord here. Then I became too closely involved in human matters for the liking of my kin. And I was foolish enough to fall in love with a korrigan lady, and attempt to win her to me with human arts. I was exiled and told I could only come back to *mabrokorr* if I agreed to scout for those talented humans who might benefit from time spent in our lands.'

'Or who might benefit you!' said Viviane, harshly. 'You were known as a good man in our world, Sir Gwazig: how could you repay our trust by snatching children from all that they had known?'

'It is not always *snatching*, as you say,' said Gwazig, with a touch of fire. 'The human world is full of weeping, and it can be better for children to come with us, to dwell immortally in the korrigan lands, than to stay to face a mortal life full of sorrow and pain.'

'You give them no choice,' snapped Viviane. 'It is one thing to take grown people – to lure them, or persuade them – though even that is wrong. But to take a child! Are you not ashamed?'

Gwazig stared at her. 'Shame, lady? That is not an emotion we korrigans should feel . . . You know that. You are a Guardian.'

'I became a Guardian from choice,' Viviane said, bitingly. 'I was not horribly transformed to become so.'

Gwazig nodded, sadly. 'I . . . I have perhaps been too long in the human world, and so I . . . I . . . I do understand what you say. I did my work at first without thinking of it: all my thoughts concentrated on returning home. Home! It ate at my heart. Cannot you understand?' His eyes pleaded with her, but she hardened her heart.

165

'So you sacrificed children to this homesickness of yours.'

'No! No! Understand, I changed . . . I . . . I very soon realised what it meant. I did not want to do it any more. I started to . . . to trick my brother, by pretending that those with talents didn't really have them, by weaving webs of deception . . . And I also tried to cast my thoughts wide, to see places he might want me to target, to find suitable children, and tried to veil them. That is how I came to see Raguenel, in my mind . . . and the children.'

Viviane stared at him.

'I saw that they were highly talented, each in their own way. But I saw they were well-protected, by a good Guardian. I saw also that the Queen of the korrigans there would never agree to take the children, that she had a treaty with you. I sent a message to Rouanez. But it was too late, for my brother, who suspected me already, had learnt of Raguenel himself. And though he . . . though in the normal way of things we should not have taken him from outside the human realms that border our lands . . . Bubo saw so much potential in Gromer he was prepared to risk Rouanez's wrath. I tried to tell him he must not – I thought it foolhardy, and dangerous, and told him so. But he did not listen. Why should he? I was suspect in loyalty, and exiled in *mabroden*, a world he despises. But I was summoned back here, to teach Gromer, and given to understand that if I succeeded in this, all my past offences would be forgiven. I agreed, because, oh how the yearning of home weighed on me! I wanted to be a true korrigan again, to chase pity and tenderness from my heart. But alas, I had been irrevocably changed. I could not help seeing how unhappy the boy was, how all his strength would one day fade, because his heart was not in it, because his soul was going far in, too deep to be reached. So after a while, I . . . I refused to do any more. Bubo was angry. And when he is angry—' He sighed, and she knew what he meant.

'So he transformed you—'

'He acted rashly. He always does. He does not always intend harm. He is . . . a creature of whim. And in our countries it can be a mark of honour to bring up truly great human foster-children. You know that we do not always hold them forever; most we simply release back into the world—'

'But always with your mark on them!' she cried. 'Always with your taint—'

'Taint or gift,' he replied, sadly. 'It depends how you look at it. Isn't that so, lady?'

He broke off, looking deep into her eyes. She looked away.

'And for some,' he went on, 'it is as you say: they are never happy, always restless afterwards in their own world. For others, it deepens them, makes them . . . special. I do not know how it will be, with these two . . . They both have so much potential.'

'They had a home,' said Viviane, bitterly. 'You should understand that, you of all beings!'

'I do,' he said, very quietly. 'I do. You . . . you love them. But if you do love them, you might listen to what I have to say, without condemning me.'

She looked at him in silence. She was remembering the stories that had been told of Bonemender, of how he had helped so many cripples, how he had gentled birds (and no wonder, if he came from a bird-korrigan realm), and thought he had at least done some good in the human world. And he had said he had turned against the idea of taking children himself. Balanced with that was the idea of his living a double life; amongst people who trusted him, and had affection for him, he had been a kind of spy, who had betrayed their welcome . . . It was a difficult thing to understand, to put together.

At last, she said, as coolly as she could, 'And what good might it do, my listening to you?'

'Because I want to put things right. This has been a bad thing from the start. And it started because of the foolish rivalry between Bubo and Rouanez. They were supposed to be married, did you know that? Marry, and hold their lands in common. But Rouanez refused. She is a stiff-necked thing . . . She says she will never marry him. But he will never give up. He tries to prove to her that his realm is greater than hers, that she would do well to see that, that he is offering her more than she could offer him. It has led to a competition, a rivalry such as we have not seen for a long time in *mabrokorr*.'

'Oh, my lord,' said Viviane, tiredly. 'But what do these quarrels have to do with us, good sir? Why should we suffer for your lords' and ladies' squabbles?'

'I understand that. I have lived long in the human world, lady, and know things most korrigans do not. But I also know my own world well . . . and I can tell you that I am not the only one who is unhappy at this state of affairs, and who thinks it has gone on long enough.'

'Well, I'm glad of that,' said Viviane, ironically. 'But what good will that do for us?'

'Do not think you can defeat Bubo by using the magic you know. Do not directly challenge him, for he will only put a spell on you. Rouanez will soon be coming here too, and she is very angry, for she thinks Bubo is cheating her. Do not attempt to challenge her either. Remember this . . . even the bird of prey can be caught by a song like his, trapped by a tug in the right place—'

He broke off, suddenly. Viviane turned to see what had silenced him: and saw a tall, handsome man, flanked by Gromer, coming swiftly towards them.

'Dame Viviane.' The handsome man bowed. He was even more handsome close up, ageless, with centuries of cool intelligence in his golden eyes, and long black hair, as glossy as Gromer's, flowing over his shoulders on to the magnificent owl's feather cloak he was wearing. On Viviane's shoulder, Estik shuddered, while Gwazig seemed to shrink into his transformed being.

The Archduke held out his hands – slim, long-fingered, long-nailed, beringed – in greeting. 'I am Archduke Bubo, lord of this realm. You are most welcome.' His eyes fell on Estik, who shrank back further still. Bubo's lips curved in a predatory, amused smile. 'And you, too, little thing.'

Not waiting for an answer, he went on, 'Has my brother been regaling you with sad stories, Dame Viviane? Pay no heed to him; he has not been quite himself since he came back to *mabrokorr*.'

Dame Viviane bit her lip, suddenly hating the casual cruelty of the glance the Archduke bestowed on his unfortunate brother, but remembering Gwazig's warning, she said nothing.

'Will you do me the honour, Dame Viviane, of allowing me to escort you into my home?' Bubo glanced laughingly at the blank-faced Gromer. 'Gromer may not know you yet, Dame Viviane, but there is another inside who will know you well. We know her as Ragnell-girl. You may know her by another name.'

A wild hope surged in Viviane. 'Is it Tiphaine?' she whispered, unable to stop her voice from shaking. The Archduke waved a languorous hand. 'As I said, we call her Ragnell-girl; you may call her another name. But take care, Dame Viviane; the sight of her may shock you. Rouanez has not been as good a Guardian to her as I have been to Gromer.'

Viviane's heart thumped as she remembered the vision at the Lake. She glanced at Gromer who stared back unseeingly at her. Something had been done to him too, despite Bubo's words. Something terrible; worse even than Gwazig's transformation, or what she feared had been done to Tiphaine. Something that had changed him inside; that no longer connected him to his human identity. She remembered Gwazig's words, and shivered inwardly. He was strong, handsome, powerful-looking, her Gromer, now; he had grown from a boy to a man, and he had a presence as strange and potent as a star come to earth. But no human warmth shone in his eyes; he was as perfect as the most perfect of the korrigan kind, but without even their brittle vitality and quicksilver nature. He might as well have been made of stone. He had been *hollowed* . . . Hollowed, in the hollow lands . . .

But all Viviane said was, 'Well, lord Bubo, what are we waiting for? I am eager to speak with Tiphaine.'

170

'Very well. Don't say I haven't warned you,' said the smiling Archduke, and taking her arm, he led her into the castle, with Gromer trailing silently in their wake. But Gwazig stayed where he was, looking after them, shoulders hunched and strange head bowed.

Nineteen

*T*iphaine saw Viviane before the old lady saw
her, and would have tried to creep out of the
way if she'd been able to move. She and Gwengan
had been brought into the main audience-chamber of
Bubo's castle only moments before, and had come face
to face with Gromer again. She had only just been able
to stop from flinging herself at the young warrior and
crying out his name; but something deep inside her,
something she had learnt while in Rouanez's realm,
told her this would be very unwise. So she held her
tongue; held it so strongly that it felt like lead in her
mouth. But she could not stop her eyes from fastening
hungrily on the tall man who was her twin, and that
gaze had told her the worst. Gromer had indeed had
his *daouden* taken from him; or else it was somewhere
deep inside him, too far to reach. The fiction she had
told to Rouanez about Alain now seemed to burn in
her brain; how ghastly it was that she had somehow
anticipated the true fate of her brother! A treacherous
thought came to her, then, about Alain; but it only
flickered briefly into life, and died down again in an

instant. No. She was not going to propose bargains, a life for a life, a soul for a soul. Bubo must be made to free Gromer; but Alain would not be sacrificed in exchange, to either him or Rouanez or any other korrigan.

Gromer left the room. Behind her ear, the lizard moved not at all, but she was aware of its tiny heart beating, blending with the beat of her own blood. She felt ashamed and despondent.

'Well, now are you happy we're in lord Bubo's country?' The harsh voice of Gwengan broke into her thoughts. Tiphaine looked down at the *duz*. There was a nasty smile on his face.

'You don't look too happy, Ragnell-girl. And yet we're back in *mabrokorr*!'

'Yes, and Rouanez is on her way to deal with you,' snapped Tiphaine. 'Don't think because we're here, you'll be able to sneak behind my back. Remember the words of binding I put on you.'

'How can I forget?' sneered the *duz*. 'You said them as well as any korrigan. Ah, Ragnell-girl, you're hardly human any more, inside or out!'

It stung. Tiphaine was searching for words to answer, when Viviane came into the room, with the korrigan lord Tiphaine remembered from that fateful day in Stone Wood. But it was Viviane, not Bubo, who made Tiphaine's heart leap in her chest and her limbs turn to lead. Her dear Viviane! And Estik . . . She could not bear them to see her like this . . . she must run, must hide . . . But she could not move at all.

Bubo's eyes searched her out at once; and a smile curved over his face. 'Ah, Ragnell-girl,' he said, softly. 'It is welcome you are to my country.'

Estik moved on Viviane's shoulder, and made a soft little sound. But Viviane's eyes met hers, then; and the shock that immediately leapt into the old woman's face was enough to end Tiphaine's paralysis. With an inarticulate cry, she fled. Or at least she tried to flee; for she found she could not leave the room. The doorway turned to a sheet of thick glass; the windows disappeared into space; and her feet kept stubbornly bringing her back to the place where she'd started. Gwengan was shrieking with laughter, Bubo smiling thinly. But Viviane stood as if turned to stone, her eyes fixed on Tiphaine, who found that all of it, this was what hurt most, the thing she could not bear. She gave up, and sank to the floor, her head in her hands.

'What is the matter, Ragnell-girl? Does Dame Viviane frighten you? You are known to be a plucky fighter, in *mabrokorr*, and clever too – oh yes, we have been keeping an eye on you, from here – but all I see is a little girl sobbing on the floor. What is wrong with you? Aren't you, after all, come on an embassy from my great and gracious lady Rouanez?'

'She is a great fool, a great fool,' cried Gwengan, capering before the korrigan lord. 'She thought to fool you, my lord!' His eyes sought Tiphaine's, maliciously. 'I gave my binding word that I would say nothing to Rouanez, but nothing about my lord Bubo!'

'Say all you like,' said Tiphaine, after a small silence. 'I care for nothing. My brother is lost forever; my old nurse does not know me and finds me hateful in her sight. Only Estik shows me any true recognition. I do not care what you say, Gwengan. I release you of all bindings.'

As she spoke, something seemed to snap in her, some heaviness, and all at once, she felt a lightness fill her, a thing that was greater than relief yet not so hopeful, either. She felt the lizard Skilf, who had been Alain, move slightly behind her ear and heard his claws scritching warmly on her poor transformed flesh. And she heard Viviane's voice, saying, gently, 'You are not hateful to me, dearest Tiphaine. Only dear, and lovely, always.'

'I am not lovely!' shouted Tiphaine, rearing up to full height. 'Look at me! I am ugly! I am loathsome!'

'No,' said Estik, making Viviane start, for the bird was speaking aloud for the first time since the twins had been taken. 'You are neither ugly nor loathsome, just a little strange. There is the bird in you, lady,' he said, shyly, cocking his head to one side, 'and something of the girl. It is strange; but I daresay we could all get used to it—'

'Oh Estik, Estik,' said Tiphaine, in a surge of affection, 'you are a dear, sweet bird, but . . . but I know Dame Viviane does not really feel the same, though she loves me, and seeks to make me feel better by saying I am lovely. I am loathsome, dear Estik, in the eyes of the human world: I can never, ever return there—'

At that moment, she saw Gromer's eyes turning to her: fixed on her as they were now, the emptiness within them seemed even more complete. She could not help shrinking back from it.

Viviane touched her gently on the shoulder. 'You will return, if I can have anything to do with it,' she said, softly. Turning to Bubo, she said, in a very different voice, 'My lord, is it that in this *mabrokorr*, all honour, all kindness, has been lost? You said that I would be shocked to see my darling Tiphaine; and indeed I was, but not for the reason she thinks. I am only a human being, Lord Bubo, and you are a great korrigan lord; but I am also a Guardian, and have the right to speak freely in *mabrokorr* as much as in my own world. Hear this, then. I am shocked because of the cruelty of what has been done to her. And what has been done to Gromer. You say that you were a better Guardian to Gromer than Rouanez was to Tiphaine. And yet you have taken his *daouden* from him, and turned him into a sleepwalker without a soul. What kind of Guardian could he be, like this? You have laid waste to any true talent he had, trying to force him too quickly into a role he neither understood nor mastered!'

'Stay,' broke in Bubo, his golden eyes narrowing. 'You do not know the full story. You do not know that it was not I who took Gromer's *daouden* from him: how could I do that? I am no demon! He chose for himself to exile it far from him.'

'For himself? I have never heard of anyone but a sorcerer doing that and—'

'Then you do now,' he said, sharply. 'That is a measure of his power, Lady Viviane. And of his sister's. Ask her what she has done with her *daouden*.'

Viviane looked at the startled Tiphaine, then back to Bubo. 'I will not ask her,' she said, tightly, though her heart raced. This was indeed the most dangerous case she had ever encountered. 'I know they are not sorcerers.'

'Who said they were?' said Bubo, crossly. 'You humans can be so limited. What they have done to try and defeat and bamboozle us, see you, is a measure of their power, their talent.' He sounded almost admiring, thought Viviane, confused by his constant changes of mood. Bubo read her expression, and smiled. 'And as to the esteemed Queen of my heart – Rouanez could have chosen to tell Ragnell-girl any time she chose, just what could be done to lift her disguise, and—'

'No disguise,' burst out Tiphaine, the anger and pent-up grief of years making her fearless, 'but a wicked enchantment put on me by you, lord Bubo!'

He was still smiling. 'A plucky fighter indeed,' he said. 'And I admit, it was a rash thing to do. But you made me cross, Ragnell-girl. What else could I do?'

She stared at him, at his bright shallow eyes, his quicksilver features, and her heart sank. 'My lord . . . if you admit it was a rash thing to do, will you not . . . please . . . lift the enchantment from me?'

'Can't,' he said at once. 'What's done is done.'

'Yes, Lord Bubo,' said Viviane, her eyes fixed on him, 'you said there was something Rouanez could have told Tiphaine to do to . . . transform the spell—'

'The right question must be asked of Ragnell-girl,' said Bubo promptly. 'It must be asked, not by a korrigan, but by a human. And no,' he said, raising a hand, 'I cannot tell you what it is. That you will have to find out for yourself.'

They always gave with one hand, took with the other.

Tiphaine's heart was full of bitterness. She said, low, 'What possible use was it to you, or to the Queen, to keep us both? What possible gain have you received from it? Neither of you has gained one thing, as far as I can see.'

Bubo's lips tightened. 'You will be able to ask the

Queen yourself that, Ragnell-girl,' he said coldly. 'She is on her way here.'

'But you, sir,' persisted Tiphaine, 'why will *you* not answer me?'

'It is not your role to ask questions,' hissed Bubo. 'You do not know what you are meddling with.' There was a small silence, then he went on, in an irritable voice, 'Yet I, for my part, because I admit I was rash, and because I admire your fighting spirit, am willing to grant you a boon. Just to show I bear you no ill feeling.'

'Any boon?' said Tiphaine, quickly, and she saw Viviane's face change as if she could sense the direction of Tiphaine's thoughts. Gromer . . .

'Any boon: within reason, apart from changing your looks,' said Bubo.

Gwengan interrupted, squeaking, 'My lord, my lord, you have not heard from me, what she was going to do!'

'Be silent, *ðuz*!' Bubo's voice was suddenly as harsh as it had been light before.

'But my lord, she —'

Bubo's voice rang like thunder. 'Be silent, *ðuz*!' And he whirled in his splendid cloak on the *ðuz*, whirling faster and faster. And as he did so, it seemed to Viviane and Tiphaine that he was changing, transforming into a gigantic, magnificent owl, an owl with the stare and beak of an eagle, with the restless, cold, murderous fury of the arch-predator in its golden eyes. And Gwengan himself was dwindling, dwindling, transforming too, his terrified squeak becoming that of the mousey creature clutched now in the owl's enormous claws.

Tiphaine acted without thought, reason or anger.

She cried out, 'A boon, lord Bubo, you said I could have! Spare the life of the *ðuz*, lord Bubo, I ask of you, I bind you to give!'

As she spoke, it seemed to her that the whole world shattered around her; she could hear howls and screams and weeping, and above it, the wild yell of the most triumphant predator of them all, fate with its inescapable laws. And she knew she had given away her one chance to free her brother for the life of a worthless *ðuz* who had tried to betray her. If she could have, she would have taken her words back. But she could not. And she could not even weep. She could only stand, dry-eyed, dry-hearted, as the owl turned back into Bubo and Gwengan, *ðuz* again, lay collapsed on the floor, shaking and shivering. She knew Viviane was standing staring at her, but she could not look. She heard a strange sound from somewhere, but did not want to know what it was. She did not attempt to speak to any of them, but turned on her heel and headed for the doorway. And this time, the space stayed space, and she was able to step through it, and away, out of the audience chamber, out through the courtyard, out of the castle, and out into the meadows beyond.

She walked and walked, her ears ringing with her own words, her body light as dust, as a feather blown on the wind, her heart unanchored. She had failed. She would always fail. She had hoped Viviane and Estik might be able to help – but how could they? The korrigans had her and Gromer like rats in a trap; or rather, mice on a treadmill. And she had ensured it would always be so . . . Even the gentle presence of Skilf at her ear did not make her feel better.

At length, she stopped, and flung herself on the grass under a particularly beautiful apple tree. But she did not notice the beauty, because in *mabrokorr* it was always around you, and there was no filth or decay to make you appreciate how rare and sweet beauty was. Only she was ugly and loathsome; and stupid as well. She groaned, deeply, and, wrapped in her silk cloak, its hood over her head, she lay on the grass, face full into the perfume of it, and felt her heart breaking. She knew this was the end. She would never go home. And neither would Gromer. As to Alain . . . he would be a prisoner too. It had all been for nothing.

All at once, she heard whisperings behind her.

'No, I think she's not . . .'

'You think we should ask?'

'She might be angry—'

They were speaking in Breton. She groaned again. Just go away, she prayed. Go away, whoever you are. You don't want to see me. And I don't want to see you.

'Lady—' A hesitant touch at her shoulder. 'Please. We need help. Directions—'

'Can't help,' she muttered, voice muffled. 'Can't—'

'You speak Breton!'

Too late, Tiphaine realised what she'd done. She stammered, 'All korrigans know Breton . . .'

'But not with your accent, lady! Are you a human, lost like us in korrigan country?' There was a lightness, a happiness to the voice that surprised her.

'That I am,' she sighed, her heart racing a little. 'Lost in *mabrokorr*, for so long—'

'Have you seen one of us – a young boy, our friend, who has been taken by the korrigans and brought to this place by two korrigans – a bird-hag and a *duz*?'

180

Tiphaine was silent an instant. Then she said, very gently, 'He is with me.'

'With you!'

'Yes, with me—' A wild hope surged in her. 'If . . . if I give him to you, perhaps you will be able to take him out of here!' A tiny silence, then, 'But stay: have you eaten or drunk anything here?'

'No!' came the firm reply in two voices.

'Good: have you given your word to anyone here?'

'No. We came in by accident, really, because we heard the password that the bird-hag used to get into this place.'

Tiphaine's blood was pounding in her head. A strange desperate happiness was making her dizzy. She said, 'Then you might be able to do it. Reach behind my left ear—'

She heard a dismayed silence, then a voice, the first one, robust, warm, protesting. 'But, lady, won't you stand up, let us see you, it is strange speaking like this . . . and—'

'And really, behind your left ear!' That was the other voice; light, merry, charming. It made her smile to herself, then she remembered who she was, and how they must not see her, or her heart would break all over again.

'Yes . . . please believe me. It was the only way I could think of protecting him . . . He is in the form of a little lizard, behind my left ear.'

'A lizard!' The first voice had a smile in it too. 'Well, I suppose little Alain always liked lying in the sun—' A finger delved behind Tiphaine's ear, very gently, delicately, found Alain, and gently took him out.

'The charm usually lasts only a day,' said Tiphaine,

muffled still. 'But I . . . a little too much of it was used, so it may take up to a week to wear off. You will have to take care of him while he is in this shape. Any bird can make a meal of him,' she added, shivering, thinking of all the handsome people in their feather cloaks, and of Bubo transforming into an owl. 'Take good care of him.'

'We will, lady.' The light voice. 'But how did you . . . the bird-hag—'

For the second time that day, Tiphaine acted without reason, thought or anger. 'I *am* the bird-hag,' she said, and slowly sat up. She looked up at them, waiting for their cries of horror. She saw a plain-faced young man, with deep, sorrowful eyes, and a handsome young man with a sparkling countenance, holding the lizard in the palm of his hand. She had seen both of them before, in the forest of Stone Wood. Then, they had recoiled from her, as if at the sight of a demon. Now, they looked steadily at her, with recognition but no horror in their eyes. Nobody exclaimed. No-one cried out. No-one said anything. They all just stood and looked at each other.

Then Tiphaine sighed, and said, 'I must go . . . Back to the castle. They will be waiting for me there. You must leave now, before Rouanez comes, and she will be here soon. You know the password; and the Guardian will not touch you, because Bubo has no interest in any of you, and does not even know Alain exists. But Rouanez wants him, and she will not let you go, once she knows. So hurry away, and do not return.'

The handsome-faced young man said, simply, 'Thank you, lady. We will never forget you.'

But the plain man said, gently, 'Stay, lady – what is your name?' In his eyes was something that Tiphaine had not seen for such a long time that she did not know what it was, but that sent a strange sweetness fizzing along her veins.

'Tiphaine,' she answered, after a while. 'I am Tiphaine de Raguenel.'

His eyes widened. 'But Raguenel – I know of the Raguenels! Their children . . . their children were taken by the korrigans!'

Tiphaine nodded, and bent her head, so he wouldn't see the tears welling in her eyes. 'That was my brother Gromer and I.'

'And they did this to you, lady Tiphaine! Why? Why?'

'Whim,' said Tiphaine, lightly. 'They act without thought, just because they want to. For Gromer, they did not change his face, only his heart. He has none, any more. They made him lose his *daouden*. He is the Guardian you saw at Dergwenn.'

'But that is monstrous!' The plain young man's face had darkened. 'How can we help you defeat them?'

'Help me?' Tiphaine smiled. 'Defeat them? You cannot help me. You cannot defeat them, any more than you can defeat the wind, or water, or fire, or the stars. They act without deliberate evil, only indifference to our needs, only thoughtlessness, only unpredictability. All you can do for us now is to please, leave quickly, with Ski . . . with Alain. My heart will be lightened, knowing he is going home, that he will not be trapped in *mabrokorr*, as I was. Please, I beg of you, leave at once. Please. That is the only way you . . . you can help me.'

They looked at her, gravely. Then the plain-faced young man spoke firmly. 'We will leave, lady Tiphaine, because you asked us to. But we will return. And that time, we will not leave this place without you. And your brother.' He reached out a hand to her. 'My name is Bertrand du Gwezklen, lady. I am of the country of Broceliande. Merlin was of our land. They will never defeat us, never fear.'

It was not his fighting words, but the warm human touch of his hand that made the blood sing in Tiphaine's veins, as it had not done so for oh, such a very long time! For the first time, real hope leapt in her. 'I thank you,' she murmured, brokenly. 'I thank you.'

'Thank us when we've done it,' smiled the other young man, and in his merry eyes was a gentleness that almost undid Tiphaine. 'Wat Davies at your service, lady. And from a fighting breed too, in the borderlands; what's more, we say Merlin was of *our* lands!' he added, lightly, smiling at his friend, who shrugged good-humouredly. Tiphaine swallowed. This lightness of being, this easy friendship – how long was it since she had known, or even *seen* either thing?

'We will go now, lady, to put Alain in safety. But we will return,' said Bertrand, and bowed deeply to her. But his eyes never left her face, and her blood sang again.

'Goodbye, Bertrand and Wat,' she said softly. 'You have already done me more good than you can know. But take care. Take great care, for when you return, it will not just be the people here – Archduke Bubo's people – but those of Rouanez you will have to face. And those two combined—' Her heart missed a beat as

184

she thought of it. 'It will be much more dangerous than you can even imagine.'

'We will remember that,' said Wat, smiling again; and the thought came to her that the young man was enjoying himself. Enjoying himself! It made her scalp crawl. His innocence: did he not understand the powers of the korrigans? She was about to say something, when, carried light on the wind, came a sound that made her freeze: a silvery trumpet-call. Rouanez was well on her way!

'Go, go, quick!' she called, and fled towards the castle herself, without another word. Once, she turned and looked behind her; and they had gone. Oh, how her heart tightened and sank at the knowledge they were going! How could they really return and help her and Gromer? How could they? It was only then that the thought struck her, with a dull surprise: why hadn't they recoiled at the sight of her? Why had there been no horror in their eyes? Her pulse quickened. Bubo had said if someone asked the right question . . . and they had asked several, those two young men. Could it be that . . . but just then, she came into the hall, passing a window, and the tiny hope withered and died in her. Reflected back at her was a loathsome, unnatural figure: herself, unchanged from the form she'd had to live in for so many years.

Twenty

'*I* knew her voice,' said Bertrand. 'It was her.' His plain face was transfigured with wonder, alight with passion and tenderness. 'It was her voice, Wat; the girl I heard in Stone Wood. How dreadful it must have been for her, seeing us recoil from her then! She was horribly transformed, and a prisoner of the korrigans; and we did not help her—'

'Be reasonable,' said Wat. 'How could we know? The bird-hag was ugly enough to frighten off a legion of demons, even. She should have told us then.'

'She could not,' said Bertrand, softly. 'She was under the korrigans' power.'

'She still is,' said Wat. 'And we will be soon enough, if we're not swift . . . Hark! What was *that*?'

That was the sound of the trumpet, closer this time. The two young men looked at each other. Bertrand jerked a thumb upwards. 'I'm going up this tree,' he said. 'I'm not leaving Tiphaine to her fate. You take Alain, Wat, and make yourself scarce. At least one of us will get out . . . Ow! Oh!'

The lizard had moved from his palm, with lighning

186

swiftness up his arm, up his sleeve, to his ear. There, it moved restlessly around, tickling Bertrand dreadfully. Its little claws went scritch, scritch, scritch; scritch. 'What are you trying to—'

At that moment, there was a little whir of wings. Estik had landed on Bertrand's shoulder. The lizard scrabbled desperately, Bertrand howled and hit out at the bird, Wat reached out to beat it off.

No, no! Listen to me!' The nightingale's voice was thin, rusty, heavily accented, so that the two youths could hardly understand it, and had to strain to listen. 'Viviane say this. She understand what to do. You must bring him—'

'Bring who?'

'The singer! They will not be able to resist. Bird of prey must be caught with own song. You hear that, lizard thing?' Estik went on, cocking his head to where Skilf crouched timidly.

Bertrand frowned. 'But Tiphaine said—'

'You listen to Viviane! She older, understand more. And she speak to one who knows truth. You bring him. He come to no harm. You will escape, and take them with you. But you must be strong.'

Their heads were whirling. 'But how do we—'

'Up the tree,' snapped the nightingale, and suited action to the word, flying up into the branches where it hid behind a particularly fat apple. Bertrand and Wat didn't wait to hear any more; they scrabbled up into the branches, Skilf-Alain still clinging on in that dreadful ticklish manner behind Bertrand's ear.

They were only just in time; for a procession soon came into view: first, a dwarf blowing a silver trumpet, followed by korrigan soldiers marching two by two, then, a golden velvet and silken litter carried swaying on the shoulders of several strapping soldiers. In it, just visible through half-parted curtains, was a woman of extraordinary beauty, with long flowing black hair and eyes as green as the sea, dressed in shimmering green and gold and blue robes, a crystal circlet holding down a translucent golden veil on her shining head. Behind her came still more korrigans, of all shapes and sizes and colours, like a flowing, multicoloured sea undulating over the land.

Wat and Bertrand held their breath as the procession passed below them. When they had gone, Wat clutched Bertrand's arm. 'Did you see her? Did you?'

'What?' said Bertrand, whose mind was working fast and furiously. So this was Rouanez, Queen of the korrigans. He remembered the *duz* calling on her when Alain was captured. She did not look dangerous – but she must be, like all korrigans.

'We must hurry,' said the nightingale, breaking into his thoughts. 'If we have chance of saving the children without incurring anger of Otherworld.'

'I'm not sure how the two can go together,' said Bertrand, climbing down the tree, but Estik replied, 'It can be done, if the right thing is done.'

Wat was silent as they hurried in the wake of the procession towards the castle. Bertrand didn't think this strange; there was, of course, a great deal to think about. He wished that Estik would be less annoyingly gnomic about what had to be done: singing didn't seem helpful, and 'the right thing' could be anything at all. Besides, what he was thinking about most of all was Tiphaine; about the depth of sorrow she must have had to face, all these years, and how he could, if not change that, at least make it bearable.

Bertrand had never imagined any woman would love him, as a woman loves a man; and he had never dreamt of it, being a practical and realistic person who knew he had too many handicaps to ever be the object of a woman's desire. But he had loved in silence, once or twice, from afar; and now, he knew that he loved again. He had fallen in love with a dream, with a woman's voice, and now with the knowledge of her sorrow, bravely borne, her tenderness towards Alain, her bravery. The loathsomeness of form truly meant nothing to him, because at the moment he had heard her, the scales had fallen from his eyes. He would love her as the woman in his vision or as the bird-hag that had stood before him; he would love her because she was who she truly was. He could not have explained this to anyone, and did not intend even to inflict it on Tiphaine. He would do his utmost to help her, but make no demands. She had suffered greatly; that was enough.

'Now, then,' whispered Estik, as they drew near to the castle, 'you will have to listen carefully to what I say. Before the gates, you find a man, a man of Bubo's kind but not his heart. You know him already.'

'We do?' said Wat, quizzically.

'Yes. He will tell you what thing it is you must do. Then you must reach the lady Tiphaine, and obtain from her one thing: the one hair she took from her brother's head. It is then up to you, and to the singer.' Gently, he tapped with his beak near Bertrand's ear, where the little lizard lay coiled, unmoving.

Wat said, 'You mean that Alain has to sing?'

'Of course,' snapped the nightingale. 'Isn't that what I told you before?'

'But Tiphaine wanted us to—'

'She does not know. She does not understand. The right question has not been asked, so she is not fully herself.'

'The right question?' said Bertrand, his heart hammering loudly.

'That is how she will be freed from her spell,' said Estik. 'I heard Bubo say it. Someone must ask her the right question. And do not ask me which it is, or it will not be right. I know it is not me that must ask it.'

Viviane was not afraid of korrigans. She knew them well. She did not underestimate them, either, though: she knew they could pass in a moment from sweet friendliness to cold fury, from good cheer to the surliest rage. It was as well, when one was anywhere near them – but especially in their territory – to remember that the only predictable thing about the korrigans was their unpredictability. In their realm, an ordinary person might well feel overwhelmed. But Viviane was no ordinary person. She had her own tricks. She could see at a distance, for instance, by concentrating on an image in her mind: and knew thus that Bertrand and Wat were hiding somewhere in this place. Here, too, she also had an ability to catch at some of the stray thoughts of the korrigans, that clung like gossamer around them. This had been the reason why she had been able to construct the shield around Ti-Korriganed.

Now, she had heard Rouanez's silver trumpet call, and knew it for that of the Queen of the korrigans of Stone Wood. And that had made her heart lift, for at least with her, she was on familiar ground. Besides, as Rouanez had not been able to pierce the shield Viviane had put around Ti-Korriganed – small revenge that had been – it was perhaps possible that she would not be able to hide all her gossamer fancies from Viviane. The rivalry between Rouanez and Bubo, as Gwazig had indicated, had got beyond normal korrigan spite; this was a giant battle of wills, and Rouanez and Bubo both might be distracted by it from other things. So she thought, as she searched deftly for one coherent thought in the webs floating around her: and that was when she saw Alain. Or at least, the idea of Alain, in Rouanez's mind; and she thought she saw that Rouanez so fiercely wanted him that she might bargain away Tiphaine for the child.

Viviane did not consider for a moment really bargaining with Rouanez; unlike Gwazig, she had no korrigan blood in her. She would never deliver an unwilling person to the korrigans; and never deliver a child at all, willing or unwilling, for children could not be expected to understand the cost a fairy gift might demand of them in the future.

But there could be a way of deflecting the korrigans in some other way, by a direct appeal to their honour, or a spellbinding by the beauty that was their lifeblood. Being of the human world, Viviane loved beauty for its transience and sweetness, but also knew there must be ugliness, for else beauty was just a cold, disdainful thing.

The korrigans, in whose realm Beauty itself lay, in whose realm enchantments began, could no more understand that, than they could understand a human heart in its entirety. The part of us that is immortal, the part that creates things of beauty, that yearns eternally for the realm of Beauty, is the part that links us to the korrigans and the other inhabitants of the Otherworld. But the part of us that is mortal clay, the part that is warm and messy and slow and sorrowful and loving: they can never hold that or encompass it. It made them restless and sulky, that knowledge, and in that knowledge, they could become cruel. And so they would want Tiphaine for her beauty, but whimsically destroy it; or her intelligence, and bamboozle her at every turn. They would want Gromer for his strength of presence, and hollow his soul from him. And they would take Alain the singer for the thrilling beauty of his voice, but exile him from human ears so that his music would become thin and restless as a korrigan's heart. Taint or gift, Gwazig had said: and indeed, it was known that those who had lived in the Otherworld had qualities that made them special. But always with that taint of korrigan ice in the heart. That was the cost; that was always the cost. And yet, it wasn't just one way: the korrigans might be cold, but they had a genuine fascination about humans, they were drawn to us in a way that could hardly be understood . . .

A kind of angry pity filled her then; but she did not forget her insight. She waited till Bubo was busy with some courtier, then sent Estik out to scout the neighbourhood, and told him what to say if he should meet with the two young men. The bird was only too glad to go; the castle made him nervous. It was far too much like a giant bird-trap for his liking, and he hadn't liked the expressions in the eyes of some of the bird-korrigans he had seen hereabouts.

She was still waiting for him to come back when Tiphaine returned. Viviane went to her at once; and now Bubo broke off his conversation to stare at the two of them, an amused smile on his face.

'What, then, my ladies,' he called out, 'did you hear the trumpet of the Queen of the fairies? She comes to upbraid me for the fact I have won: for I have both Ragnells, girl and boy with me – and their Guardian as well!'

'Come here to me, Tiphaine,' said Viviane, ignoring him; 'come here, and let me hold your hand. Now, my darling Tiphaine, I have found you, and will never let you go, this time. And I will take you from here, take you home, where you will live happily.'

'But dear Viviane,' said Tiphaine, gently, the unexpected encounter in the orchard still buoying her, 'how can I go home? I no longer know where that is . . . and I cannot go there without my brother.'

Her eyes slid over to where Gromer stood at attention, at Bubo's side, his massive frame steady, his eyes empty, and the expression in her own eyes made Viviane shudder as she remembered Bubo's words. Her children had both somehow found a strength to resist the korrigans in their own lands, on their own ground, without losing their minds: but at what cost? At what cost, dear lord? Had they – had they, like Gwazig but the other way around, irrevocably changed? Was it true: could they never go home, now? A great weariness, sadness and fear filled Viviane's soul then, for she thought she had utterly failed.

Then Tiphaine spoke again. 'Go, dear Dame Viviane, take his hand, hold it, make him remember a warm human touch. A touch that has not been too tainted by the korrigans.' She touched Viviane's hand, gently, and looked into her eyes. And Viviane found herself strangely comforted, and able to do as she asked.

Tiphaine had spoken softly; but Bubo had heard. 'Tell me, Ragnell-girl,' he said, strolling over to her, 'will you be so fiery when my lady Rouanez is here?'

Tiphaine stared proudly at him, but did not answer. He came right up close to her, and looked deep into her eyes. Heat seemed to come from that gaze; a kind of melting warmth that enveloped Tiphaine's limbs; and a light played over her body that seemed to come from it. In the light of that gaze, she saw her old self, her old body, lying like a transparent shadow over her hideous present shape. She could not help but give a cry, and stumble back. Bubo came closer again.

'You please me, little one,' he drawled. 'I wonder if—' He reached out a hand and touched Tiphaine's skin, and his eyes narrowed. 'Yes. It is true. You have been changed. Not just this disguise, but underneath. You are more like one of us than your brother could ever be.'

'My lord,' said Tiphaine, speaking then out of a horror and a hope almost too great to bear, when mingled together in this way. 'If that is so – will you not let Gromer go, and keep me in his place?'

The golden gaze washed over her. Bubo said, quietly, 'I give her a boon, and she saves that wretched *∂uz*. I pay her a compliment, and she tries to sell it back to me! Do you know where Gwengan is now, lady?'

'No . . .' stammered Tiphaine, cold and hot crawling over her, together. Bubo took her hand, and idly traced along it with one long fingernail, sending little sparks and shivers up her spine. She tried to concentrate on other things, on the sight of Viviane with Gromer, on the hope that somehow the old lady might be able to reach her brother. But his touch of fire and ice melted into her, sending shocks of fierce delight in every bit of her body.

'Look, my dear, look where your kindness has led,' he said, gently, and motioned towards the doorway. And there, a frightened yet spiteful-looking Gwengan at her side, stood Rouanez, Queen of the korrigans of Stone Wood. And she was certainly not in the best of tempers.

Twenty-One

*B*ertrand could hardly believe his ears. The hermit he had liked and spoken with in Broceliande, the fearless man who had been respected and trusted by the people around him – he was a korrigan lord! The fact of Gwazig's hideousness had no bearing on that, except as something to pity him for, and to hate Bubo more for; but the idea that all these years, Gwazig had been acting as 'scout' as he put it, was almost too much to bear. Bertrand stared at the creature before him, unable to frame even a civil word. It was Wat who had to do most of the talking, and Wat who drew Bertrand aside for a few seconds, to whisper in his ear, 'Stop it, Bertrand! You'll spoil everything with your dagger looks! Can't you see, he's sorry for what he's done; and I've never, ever heard of any otherworldly one being sorry for anything.'

'What do I care for the state of his soul, if he has one?' hissed Bertrand. 'To think we lived right near that . . . that thing, is enough to make me feel sick to the stomach. He laid his hands on people, and cured them; he treated wounded birds – and all the time, he was spying on us!'

'It doesn't make the fact of his cures less, or the gentleness with which he handled birds,' said Wat, tartly. 'He had no choice. If it was you, Bertrand – if you were exiled in a strange land, and yearned for home, and were given an opportunity to work off your offence: would you not take it? I know I would.'

'I hope I would think further on what I was doing,' grumbled Bertrand.

'All very well; but have you not done things yourself you are not proud of? Besides, he said he realised soon enough, and tried to head the korrigans off. And what of now? He is the only one to know really how we can defeat the Archduke and the Queen. He is putting himself in danger, you know.'

'Hmm,' said Bertrand, and looking up, he caught Gwazig's gaze. The korrigan's expression was empty of self-pity, of pleading, of anything but a tight anxiety. And looking into those grey eyes, Bertrand knew that the anxiety was not for himself – or not much, anyway – but an anxiety to make amends, to put things right, to restore a balance that had been lost. Something shifted in him: something he could hardly explain to himself even after.

He nodded, briefly. 'Very well. I am sorry to react so harshly. But you understand it is not an easy thing to accept, or understand.' His words were not for Wat, but for Gwazig, who smiled sadly.

'I do not expect you to. I only ask you to imagine that, though at first I was eaten up only by the desire to go home, to be forgiven – that I was ready to do anything at all for that, as I . . . the longer I lived in the human world, I grew to . . . to understand it, to have a liking for the people who crossed my path. That is all I can say. I cannot ask your forgiveness, nor can you give it, for it is not you I have harmed, only those I have allowed my kind to abduct into our lands.' There was a small silence, then he went on, 'But enough of me. It is not that you need. You need the song. And it must be sung true.' Gently, he put two fingers to his coarse lips, and whistled, a note of such piercing beauty and sweetness that it made tears spring to their eyes. As the sound died away, Skilf the lizard, who had been Alain Mabig, came out from his hiding place. He ran down Wat's arm, into his hand; and with a graceful, amazing leap, he leapt across from him, on to Gwazig's flippered limb. Then he sat there, quietly, eyes on the transformed man.

Then Gwazig began singing, in a rich, warm, deep voice, and it seemed to Bertrand and Wat that as he did, whole vistas arose before them, vistas seen from a high distance: landscapes falling and rising under the beat of powerful wings, landscapes vague and formless, with, occasionally, bright sharp clear patches, filled with a pitiless silver light. It seemed to them that they could hear the high weird tones of an owl, night-hunting. It seemed to them they could hear the moon calling back to it, and the tides of the sea, and the slow roll and spin of the dark earth. It seemed to them that as he sang, head thrown back, eyes closed, Gwazig's shape was changing, so he was moving in and out of forms, now an owl, now a man, tall and broad, with silver on his brow and dark fire in his ageless eyes, now the mixed-up creature he was now. And as he sang, they became aware that another voice was joining in: a thin, silver, thrilling voice, as delightful and frightening as the light of the moon, the voice of a star come to earth . . . the voice of Alain Mabig!

Tears of ice and fire seemed to be springing out all over the bodies of the two young men; Bertrand could see Wat's face swimming with them, and he thought his must look the same. In the song was everything that linked humans to the korrigans: the song of separation from the heavens, the cry of savage joy to be alive, the love of beauty, the delight in music, the terrifying spell that might plunge you headlong into madness, or forward into great understanding, wisdom and creative power. It was both warning and invitation, call and defiance. The two voices woven together – the human child's, with its sweet, unearthly tones, and the korrigan prince's, with its warm, almost human depths – made something wondrous and awesome. And listening to its beautiful mosaic made Bertrand and Wat both understand what they must do, separately and together.

The song ended. There was a silence. The lizard who was Alain ran up Gwazig's arm, shoulder, up to his ravaged face. Carefully, then, a little tongue flicked out, and touched first the lips, then the nose, the eyes, then the ears, and so on down the creature's body till once again it was at its feet. Then the lizard scurried over to Bertrand, and climbed up his legs to his waist, his arm, and sat on his shoulder, where it perched, bright-eyed.

Something was happening to Gwazig. Something frightening and terrible: for he was cracking open, like an egg, like a hollow statue. His skin was peeling off, his flippers falling off like withered fruit, everything melting off him, dissolving, breaking. The two young men could not move; they were rooted to the spot with horror. Yet, as they watched, all at once they saw a most amazing and beautiful thing: for from the wreckage of the creature that Gwazig had become, a form was emerging: the form of a man something like the one they had seen in the song's visions, and something of the man Bertrand had known, in the forest of Broceliande. Gwazig's long hair was black and silver, his eyes shining silver and grey, and filled with an expression you would never expect to see in a korrigan's eyes: surprise. And his mouth was open, on words of simple, heartbreaking power: 'You were with us, once, and you have forgiven us!'

No-one answered: but Wat and Bertrand saw he was speaking to the lizard, and their hearts raced with the strangeness of it. Did Gwazig mean Alain had once been a captive of the korrigans himself? But if so, how had he . . .

'How could it be you could break this spell on me?' said Gwazig, wonderingly, to Skilf. 'I do not understand how it could happen —'

'Sir,' broke in Bertrand, his voice shaky, from all that had been happening, but still determined. 'Sir – do not forget. There are things we must do, in the lord Bubo's castle.'

'Yes. Yes. Of course.' Gwazig gathered his robes around him. His eyes were still full of that unkorrigan-like emotion, but he smiled, and all his face was lit up with it, so that he looked very handsome indeed. Then, gently, he said, 'May I, my dear?' And he lifted the lizard gently off Bertrand's shoulder, and put it carefully on his own. 'It is more than time we ended this,' he said, and motioned them to follow him.

When Rouanez had entered the castle hall, and spoken her fiery words, Bubo had laughed, and come towards her, with a languid gait.

'Spoken just like the lady of Stone Wood! Thinks she's still at home, even in someone else's hall, and can quarrel with inferiors before greeting her equals!'

Though his words were quiet, they were intended to sting; and Tiphaine saw the bright colour leap into Rouanez's pale cheek, and the lightning in her eyes. She advanced proudly on him.

'How dare you, Lord Bubo! I know exactly what you meant to do – steal from me everything – parade all your foster-things before me, and make me seem like a fool! You were in league with the Ragnell-girl; you've been so all along, haven't you?'

'My dear Rouanez.' Bubo shrugged his shoulders. 'You always did allow vanity to blind you.'

'I! Ha!' Rouanez's voice rose. 'You, the rash, foolish, stupid lord of this stupid little province; you who make a mockery of all our traditions and who think to gain advantage through that – it is you, you who most threaten everything we have always held to be true, in *mabrokorr*! You went outside your lands to take this child.' Here, she flung her hand out towards Gromer, standing stony some distance away, 'you turned him into a Guardian, which can never be, as he was unwilling, you kept your own brother as scout in *mabroden*, ignoring all precedent! You have endangered the paths between the worlds, you have upset all the balance, you've even played games with passwords and words of power which can never be changed: ha, if I didn't well know your lineage, I would think you had been tainted by human blood, human sorcerous treachery!'

'Really?' said Bubo, his lip curling. 'I think it is you, my dear Rouanez, who has done more to endanger the paths, as you put it. Do you think I don't know you were spying on me, before this? My people told me they'd seen you flitting about in *mabroden* when you should not have been.'

Viviane held her breath, thinking of what Gwazig had said, about warning Rouanez: would the Queen, in her fury, tell the Archduke what had happened? But she need not have worried: the korrigan Queen's pride would never allow her to admit someone might have helped her. Rouanez snapped, 'I was right to distrust you! If I could have stopped you —'

'And your taking of the Ragnell-girl,' Bubo went on relentlessly, 'taking her when you didn't even really want her, when you had no plan for her, unlike me, with her brother; that made the *strobinella* put up a barrier in Stone Wood that you could not cross. You didn't even use her talents, you didn't even try to mould her into anything useful.'

'She couldn't be made use of,' said Rouanez, coldly. 'I saw that soon enough: she was far too strong for me to mould. As her brother was, and you were too stupid and arrogant to see it.'

Bubo's eyes flashed, but he said, 'Now your hankering after the singer boy has all the hallmarks of your foolish impulsiveness, your blind grasping at traditions to further your own aims! Look at you, with that worthless *ɒuz* by your side – can't you see he was ready to betray you for a bit of imagined gold?'

'I do not need you to tell me such things,' said Rouanez, and she gave such a withering look to Gwengan that the creature shrank visibly. 'But the boy, the little one – is that why you took his *ɒaouɒen* from him?' hissed Rouanez. 'Because you could not bear me to have more than you? He was once in your lands, wasn't he?'

Now, all this time, Tiphaine and Viviane had been standing silently. But now Viviane burst out with, 'What do we care for your quarrels, oh Queen, oh Archduke? Wrong was done to my children five years ago; and that wrong must be righted.'

Now she had their attention: their full, fierce-eyed, lightning-hot attention. She swallowed, but went on, 'I am a Guardian. I have a right to speak. You both know full well that what has happened was something that should never have happened. I have always had good dealings with your realm, Queen Rouanez,' she said, and bowed in that angry lady's direction, 'and have always dealt fairly with you. The children were lured to Ti-Korriganed, at a time when according to all honour and all precedent they should have been safe.'

'That was not I,' broke in Rouanez, 'but that one over there!'

Viviane said, firmly, 'That may be so. However it happened, *both* have been kept for no good reason. My poor Tiphaine has been deformed, my poor Gromer made mad. In the old days, it was always thought that the gifts of the korrigans might outweigh the terror of being kept in *mabrokorr*. I do not see that here. I see only pain and suffering on their side; and ugly fighting and stupid rivalry on yours.' Her voice stung like a whip. 'After this day, I never want to be a Guardian. I want nothing more to do with korrigans. You have become unstable and treacherous and dishonourable as demons.'

The looks on the faces of both rulers would have been amusing, if it hadn't been so frightening. Tiphaine knew, instinctively, with the experience of five long years in *mabrokorr*, that the korrigans would not see Viviane's courage as that, but as a deadly insult that must be expunged. As Gwazig had said, they did not know shame; they would hear only words that angered them, because they were not ones they wanted to hear, and they would want to destroy the speaker of those words. Before they could complete the movements that would be the beginning of a terrible spell, she leapt forward.

'Queen Rouanez, Archduke Bubo, do not listen to this foolish, deluded old woman.' She did not look at Viviane's bewildered face, but hurried on, 'She is simply overwhelmed by her first real experience of *mabrokorr*, and seeks to make herself bigger than she really is. She is nothing: forget her. It is I you should be looking at. It is I who is thwarting you: I who has hidden the boy so well neither of you will ever find him, I who spellbound the *ðuz* so he was unable to resist my binding—' and here, she looked over at Gwengan, who shrank even further back, 'I who has bamboozled the pair of you, and neither of you even seems to know it yet!'

She drew herself up proudly, and in that moment, into her mind flashed images of the two young men she had met outside. She would never see them again, she thought, but that was no matter. They had touched her, had made her reconnect with something she had thought lost forever. She was no longer Ragnell-girl, but herself again, despite the pain, the transformation, the loss, the sorrow of seeing Gromer vanished inside himself.

'For it is I who challenge you: I, Tiphaine de Raguenel, who knows now that even if I cannot ever go back to the place I was once so happy in, that I cannot go back to my childhood, nor forget what happened to me in your lands: I know that I hold all these things within me and more. I am not afraid of you any more. And so I challenge you both now to a contest, each of you against me. If I win, I can have my brother back, and leave with all the humans. If I lose —'

'You are crying, Ragnell-girl,' said Bubo, breaking in. There was a curious look on his face. 'If you are so strong, if you are not afraid, if you think you can challenge us – why do you cry, like a weak human?'

'Because tears are not weak,' came a new voice from the doorway. 'They are a sign that in most battles with us, the humans will win.'

'Gwazig!' said Bubo, and his lip curled into a smile, as his brother, followed by Wat and Bertrand, came into the hall. 'You are back amongst us, my dear brother: and in your own shape, too! How did you accomplish this feat? And what's that little thing on your shoulder? It—'

'Enough!' shouted Rouanez. Her gaze was fixed on Tiphaine. 'I do not care to hear about your family problems, Bubo. You are truly a fool, if you do not recognise what this girl is saying. This girl I have fed and looked after for five long weary years,' she went on, pacing angrily, 'and who has never shown the slightest gratitude!' She whirled around on Tiphaine. 'I know you, my dear. You are one of us. You really, truly are. And so, if you lose this challenge, it is I who will decide on your punishment.'

'Very well, Queen Rouanez,' said Tiphaine, and she could feel the blood icing in her veins. But she kept her gaze level with the Queen's, and it was Rouanez, not Tiphaine, who first dropped her gaze. Of course, that did not improve the Queen's temper!

'And who are these fools?' she shouted, flinging an arm out at Wat and Bertrand and Gwazig. 'Can anyone wander in and out of your realm at will, Bubo? What sort of prince are you?'

'A better one than you, my dear,' said Bubo tersely, and then he turned to Tiphaine. 'I am fascinated to receive your challenge,' he said, and bowed. 'Pray tell me more.'

Tiphaine looked over him, straight into Bertrand's and Wat's eyes. In Wat's expression she read apprehension and excitement; in Bertrand's, only tenderness and pride. She swallowed, her pulse quickening. 'I challenge you to this riddle, Lord Bubo and Queen Rouanez: what is the thing that humans prize above all?'

'A riddle, eh,' said Bubo, smiling. 'A riddle!' And he smiled. Everyone else around him smiled, even Rouanez, and Tiphaine's heart sank. She had made the wrong decision . . .

This was reinforced by Bubo's next words; words which were light, whimsical, completely unthreatened. 'Very well. A riddle it shall be. A nice challenge, appreciated both by tradition . . .' (he bowed to Rouanez) 'and to mischief . . .' (he raised his eyebrows).

'Very well. A riddle on what humans prize above all. And who is to be the judge of the answers?'

'May it be I?' said Bertrand, suddenly, stepping out into full view. 'May it be I, Lady Tiphaine? Would you think me not too presumptuous if I might do so?'

She looked at him, at the feelings written in his eyes, and a strange choking feeling filled her. For five long years, no-one had asked her permission, her opinion, her feelings on anything. Korrigan ice had entered her soul, until she had come to think it normal. It hurts, when numbness begins to wear off.

She said, in a voice she tried to steady, 'I thank you, Bertrand du Gwezklen, for your kindness, and your honour. And I could scarcely think of a better man to do so. But I fear that for this riddle, we need both human insight and korrigan cleverness. We need someone who knows both, who understands both, who is of both worlds, who loves both for what is to be loved about them, but saddened by what is to be feared about them.' She looked into Bertrand's eyes. 'Do you understand?'

'I do, dear heart,' he said, softly, 'and I know why I cannot do it. But this man: Gwazig, he is one such.'

'Yes,' chimed in Wat, eagerly. 'He is exactly the one. He is one who can do such a thing.' He looked pleased, now, Viviane thought, with a little frown; silly boy, what was there to be pleased about? She did not look at Tiphaine; but her old heart was bursting with pride and love for her dear, brave girl. And with a strange, tremulous hope; a little candleflame, rising steadily.

'Gwazig!' Bubo raised his eyebrows. 'Well done, well done, my boys! You are clever, indeed. So my treacherous brother is to be judge, eh!'

'It fits,' said Rouanez, slowly. 'This is all about treachery, is it not? So it fits nicely.' She was ivory-pale again; she could be thought to be almost disdainful now, were it not for the way she bit her lips, and her restless fingers.

'Very well, then,' said Bubo. 'Let us begin this bit of fun. I think I'm already enjoying myself. Sit down, sit down, Rouanez; you look most uneasy, hovering like that. Scat, *ðuz*,' he added to Gwengan, who was showing signs of not wanting to leave Rouanez's side, but now scurried away, with a scared look at Tiphaine, who ignored him. She did not feel angry or saddened by the *ðuz*'s ingratitude; and indeed, she was not surprised. If anything, she felt a dim pity, for such a blasted, damaged, withered creature, who would never be able to stand as himself ever again. Who was she, to blame him for trying to protect himself against the korrigan rulers?

'Ask the question properly, then,' said Bubo, with a touch of impatience. 'There is a ritual about such things – isn't there, Rouanez, my dear?' he went on, leaning over to touch Rouanez's hand. 'Why don't you tell the girl what it is? May as well enjoy tradition when we can, no?'

'You are absurd, Bubo,' snapped Rouanez, but nevertheless she looked pleased. She looked at Tiphaine, and spoke in a cold voice. 'My dwarf over there will blow his trumpet. You must stand with your head flung back, and your arms wide. Your feet must be planted just so—' She broke off, frowning, as the lizard scurried down from Gwazig's shoulder, scurried across the floor, and ran swiftly up Tiphaine's arm. 'That is not in it.'

'Traditions can be transformed, dear,' said Bubo, smiling. 'Let the little creature stay.'

'Very well.' Rouanez frowned, then smiled. Her whole face lit up when she did so, and Wat gasped. She looked at him for the first time: a long, coolly assessing look. And then she smiled again, dazzlingly, and continued, while Wat's knees knocked together, much to Bertrand's amazed disgust. ('Pull yourself together, man!' he hissed fiercely in his friend's ear, to which the other replied, 'How can I? She's so gorgeous, even if she is a korrigan; or maybe especially—' Some people can't be warned, thought Bertrand, they like putting their heads in the lion's mouth.)

'You then bow to all the company,' Rouanez was saying, 'and tell your riddle. You wait a short while; then you say it again; and once more. Three times must it be said, if it is to constitute a . . . challenge, as you wish it to be!' Her lip curled.

'And then we will answer: three things can we answer, each,' said Bubo, eagerly; 'and Gwazig will listen to all the answers, and decide. So it will be done. Begin! Come on, dwarf, the trumpet!'

And so it began.

Twenty-Two

*T*iphaine's head was flung back, her feet planted wide, gaze faraway. Because she did not look at any of them there, she did not see the strange, almost awestruck expressions stealing over the humans' faces, or the raised eyebrows of the korrigans. The words of the riddle hovered on her lips; but she did not yet say them. That was because just at the moment when she'd been about to speak, a kind of panic had filled her. Did she, herself, know the answer to the question she had posed as a challenge to the korrigans? She thought that the korrigans would not be able to find the one core thing about humans, but would *she*? Had she been too long away from the human world to really know it, if she heard it? Would she know if Gwazig judged true? And if what she had half-heard, and only partly understood, about him was true, would a traitor, perhaps even a double traitor, be able to recognise or acknowledge truth when he heard it?

Truth, love, home: these had become foreign words to her. And the sense of her loss had never been as great as at that moment. She stood there in the approved korrigan manner, about to issue a ringing challenge to the korrigan world, and she was seized with that panic which was not a fear of what they might do to her, but rather of the changed being that she had become.

'Speak, Ragnell-girl! Speak!' came Rouanez's sharp voice. 'Speak, girl,' drawled Bubo. 'Speak!' squeaked, howled, shouted, yelled, hissed and murmured hundreds of korrigan voices. On her shoulder, Skilf scritched and scratched, and a thin murmur came to her: Look at us, Tiphaine, look at us! She was going to lash out at him, to ask what he meant; but then it struck her. None of the other humans had said anything at all . . .

Turning her head, Tiphaine saw that they stood all together, Bertrand, Wat, Viviane . . . and Gromer, Gromer, still holding on to Viviane's hand. His face was still blank; but he clung so fiercely to that hand that Tiphaine could see the strain on Viviane's face. Tears blinded her; and she shouted, 'I speak! I put on you a riddle, which you are bound to answer. What is it that humans prize above all?' Steadily now, strongly, she repeated the question three times. Then she stood straight, silent again, proud, tears rolling down her cheeks; eyes, heart, full of that unexpected, that glorious, wonderful sight: Gromer, not letting go of Viviane's hand.

As she watched, Bertrand, with a bashful look, took the young man's other hand; and Wat took Viviane's other hand, so they were now in an almost-circle. They looked at Tiphaine; and Bertrand held out his other hand to her, and without any interference from the korrigans, she walked towards them, took Bertrand's hand, and completed the circle, with Skilf on her shoulder.

Then Rouanez said, sharply, 'What is it humans prize most? Why, power, of course: power over the earth, power over each other, power even over the thoughts and hearts and minds of their fellows.'

'Nonsense,' snapped Bubo. 'Not all humans are sorcerers. What humans prize above all is knowledge: the knowledge to penetrate the secrets of the universe, the knowledge to understand the workings of heaven itself, the knowledge of—'

'That is just another form of power,' said Gwazig, quietly, and looking at him, where he stood a little apart from both korrigans and humans, Tiphaine saw that he looked sadder than she had ever imagined a korrigan could ever look. But Bubo sniffed.

'I did not know it was part of the ritual that you could comment on our answers,' and he looked challengingly towards Tiphaine, who murmured, with a regretful look at Gwazig, 'No, my lord, it is not. But as you yourself commented on my lady's answer, perhaps it is only right.'

'That is indeed so! You've had your first answer; it's my turn again,' snapped Rouanez, impatiently, before Bubo could speak. 'Now then: what humans prize above all, then, if it's not power, is ease. Ease to live, not to have to work too hard, ease.'

'Ha! They're not all sloths,' observed Bubo, laughing, ignoring Rouanez's annoyance. 'No; what humans prize above all is struggle. They like to challenge, to fight, to resist.' And he raised his eyebrows at Tiphaine. 'Is that not so, Ragnell-girl?'

'My lord, you have given your second answer,' said Gwazig coolly, 'and neither that one nor the other – nor my lady's one or the other – will do. There are humans who will prize each highly. But still neither is the one they *all* prize, and wish for.'

'Love, then,' said Rouanez, with a scornful air. 'Love, that turns them into fools and gulls. Love, that makes their limbs turn to water and their mouths to dust.'

'I wouldn't mind being human, for a taste of what I've heard of love,' said Bubo, with a sly look at Rouanez. 'For a slight taste of making *you* bend to me, oh esteemed Queen of my heart –'

'You are a fool!' said Rouanez, with a toss of her head. 'Don't even try to think it; I remember now what got this brother of yours exiled from this place, when he got a sorcerer to throw a love spell on a korrigan lady, as if she were a mere human! And if you try, Bubo, I swear I will curse your whole realm!' She stood straight, head held high, eyes flashing. Tiphaine saw Wat's eyes widen, heard his sigh; which he quickly hid when he saw her looking at him. But her heart was too full to worry overmuch about that. She waited for Bubo's answer.

'Why, look at you, sweet thing,' the Archduke said, lip curling, 'I can see in you the thing humans most prize: utter dignity, pride and righteousness. Never to be wrong! What a wondrous thing! Yes, Gwazig, brother undear, that's what you'll find humans most prize: dignity itself, of which their version is only a shadow, a reflection, of my lady's here!' And he burst out laughing, his shoulders heaving with mirth, seemingly unconcerned by what Rouanez had said, unconcerned too for the look of darkness gathering on Gwazig's face, and the stillness of the humans, waiting.

But Rouanez was not unconcerned. She had not forgotten what this was all about. She snapped, 'Well, Gwazig, which of those is the answer? Surely you must see it is love! Why, look at them, holding each other in that sickening fashion! Look at those fools who came blundering in here because they'd fallen in love — ' and here she pointed at Wat and Bertrand, 'the one with a dream, the one with *me*! And look what love has done for the Ragnell-girl, who because she was asked the right question by a lovelorn fool, is back to being who she was!'

Ignoring Wat's hurt look, and Tiphaine's dawning astonishment, she went on. 'And look at that old woman, wandering the earth with that stupid bird, looking for her lost children – for love! And Ragnell-girl and your false Guardian – bound by love. You must agree, Gwazig. You lived long amongst humans. You were always tainted by them, even before that. You know that is what drives them, what they want above all. Dignity! Ha! What do they care about that! What fools these mortals be!'

Gwazig looked steadily at her. 'Love is indeed a great thing amongst humans, my lady. It is indeed.' He looked at Tiphaine, but she was not looking at him, only at Bertrand: seeing, reflected in his eyes, the unutterable, astonishing fact of her retransformation: the fact she was no longer bird-hag, but a beautiful girl with a face that she hardly dare feel yet was her own . . .

A flicker of regret crossed Gwazig's face at the sight, and Bubo smiled, thinly. 'Oh Gwazig, Gwazig, brother undear, look to your answer, then.'

Nothing surprises them, thought Viviane, as her heart filled with gladness and a strange kind of pity for the korrigans. Nothing can ever surprise them. But she was wrong . . .

'That is his answer!' snapped Rouanez, now. 'It is his judgement. Love: that's what it is. That's what —'

Gwazig shook his head. 'No, my lady,' he said in a voice so soft they had to strain to hear him. 'It is something else. Something on which everything else is built, including love. Something prized above all, but often betrayed and forgotten and cast aside.'

He made a strange gesture; and Skilf, who had been Alain, leapt from Tiphaine's shoulder to the korrigan lord's; and bent close to Gwazig's ear, and raised himself on his little paws. And then Gwazig began to sing the song he had sung to Bertrand and Wat, and Alain sang with him, and the two voices, warm and deep, high and unearthly, rose together, and seemed to weave patterns of colour around them, of red and silver, gold and black, green and blue, white and amber . . . Everyone, everything was still, except for Gwazig, with Skilf on his shoulder, who, as they sang, began to dance, swaying, grasping the colours of their own song around them, pulling them around each other and the others in the hall, like skeins of living silk, weaving in and out of each other to form a living tapestry, a mosaic of colour and music and beauty that was both korrigan and human, worldly and otherworldly. And then through the song, through the living tapestry of colour came Gwazig's voice, singing words which they knew were new.

This is my answer, oh people of my kin, people of my korrigan blood. This is my answer, oh people of my exile, people of my human heart. What humans prize above all is a thing that we korrigans yearn for but rarely obtain, a thing that is often betrayed, but without which nothing can exist and nothing can be made. It is a thing small yet great, a thing of air and wishes, a thing of bone and blood. It is a thing that can be twisted, and mangled, and yet can never wholly be corrupted. It is a thing that must be given away, if it is to be loved at all, and held to; yet it can also be a chain, if it is misused. And that thing, my lords, my ladies, my dears, is trust . . .

'It is trust,' came another voice into his words, then another, then another, and another, and another ... . Trust, they whispered, trust, small and meek, yet stronger than time, stronger than the Devil, stronger than enchantment, stronger even than suffering, yet weak and small too, often mislaid, forgotten, trodden on . . . Trust, they said, on which love and honour and kindness and friendship and peace and harmony were founded; trust, which, betrayed, led to suspicion and anger and evil. None could live without it, truly; its absence blasted and withered lovers, families, villages, realms, worlds. Betrayed and misused and false-seeming trust made its name horrible, transformed it into a demonic thing, yet always, it was prized, for just as hypocrisy is the compliment vice pays to virtue, so the evil try to make trust their own.

The words died away. The dancing stopped. The colours swirled into one another, melded, then vanished. And Gwazig and Alain Mabig, lizard no more, but star-pale boy, stood facing a silent court of korrigans, a silent circle of humans. They were both smiling.

'And there you have your answer, brother; and your answer, Lady Rouanez,' said Gwazig. 'And thus all spells are ended, and none who are unwilling can be kept in *mabrokorr*; for the challenge of the lady of Raguenel, whom you called Ragnell-girl, has succeeded.'

He spoke with absolute authority. And Rouanez and Bubo looked at each other then, and nodded. Tiphaine saw – or thought she saw, for she could never be sure, with the korrigans – that something almost like tears shone in their steady gaze. Bubo said, quietly, 'You have earned your place back into our realm, brother,' and Rouanez spoke, gently. 'If it were you asked for my hand, Lord Gwazig—'

But he shook his head, and smiled. 'It was never about me,' he said. 'It was Tiphaine, and Gromer, and Bertrand, and Wat, and Viviane, and yes, little Estik. And Alain: Alain Mabig. It is they who gave me the answer, who made me see. It is they, my lord and lady, who restore balance to our lands by their very presence. For even if we korrigans do not trust each other or humans, still, we yearn for it. We seek, because we know it exists. Brother, Queen, your quarrels and my own foolishness long ago caused our world to be out of joint: and so we made theirs out of joint too. But that is over. Over. There will be no more unwilling takings, from human lands into these at least. Ever.'

The ghost of angry regret flashed across both of the korrigan rulers' faces; but then Bubo shrugged and said, 'As you wish,' and he walked to Gromer, and as if it were the most casual thing in the world, touched him on the shoulder, the eyes, the mouth. 'Unwilling never,' he said, 'but if you wish to return, you may.'

Tiphaine saw the last of the lost, empty expression leave her brother's face; she saw his bewilderment as strange memories and confusions, dammed up for five years, roared through his mind. Then he turned his gaze to hers, and a slow, tentative, delighted smile spread across his features.

'Tiphaine,' he said, in a voice that must have sounded strange even to his ears, for he started at the sound of it, 'Tiphaine: you are here?'

'I am, dear Gromer,' she said, and at last took her twin brother in her arms, small against his great bulk, he clumsily reaching down to her, and time and suffering and everything faded and dissolved for them. 'I want to go home, Tiphaine,' he murmured, and she replied, 'And I want to go with you, Gromer—'

She turned her head a little, to look into the eyes of the Queen of the korrigans, who frowned, and stalked forward, saying, 'Oh, very well! You can go home, Tiphaine, I'll allow you to.'

'Oh, but my lady,' said Tiphaine, gently, 'I never intended to stay.'

Rouanez's eyes flashed, her lips tightened; then all at once, she began laughing. 'I will be sorry to see you go, Ragnell-girl,' she said, lightly. 'Pig-headed human that you are, I can still see the quicksilver korrigan spirit working in you, and it amused me.' She touched Tiphaine on the top of her head.

'You will not have to forget all you learnt and saw,' she said. 'Not even how you saw into the *duz*'s mind,' she added, severely, darting a meaningful glance at an uneasy Gwengan. 'I will match the Archduke's promise: unwilling never, but if you wish to return, you may.'

Her voice changed, became almost pleading. 'Little one,' she said, turning to Alain, 'star-child, singer of my heart, will you, perhaps consider staying with us for a short time, to teach us your songs? I promise on all korrigan honour that you can come and go as you please in my lands—'

'And in mine,' drawled Bubo. 'What do you say, child?'

Alain smiled. 'I would like that,' he said simply, and that silenced everyone for a moment. Bertrand thought: why, heavens, maybe the child was not afraid, could have coped with the korrigans, is of the kind that is unscathed by contact with them! And Tiphaine thought, well, well – and I never even thought to ask him. But the korrigans looked unsurprised; they looked at each other, well-pleased.

'You have been with us before, I think,' said Rouanez. Alain answered, 'Not here – but in a place like it. But I got tired of it, so went back to the world.'

'Just like that!' said Wat, speaking for them all.

Alain nodded. 'Of course.'

'I knew it,' said Rouanez, with great satisfaction, but Bubo answered tartly, 'You knew nothing of the sort. You thought he was a korrigan; but he's not, he's a changeling. An inbetweener. Can live in both places, that's all.'

'Umm—' Wat cleared his throat. 'If we can't be unwilling, but—' He looked at the korrigans, blushed, tried again. 'May I . . . I'd like to . . . that is—'

'You'd like to be invited in, too?' said Bubo, raising his eyebrows. Rouanez smiled. 'Very well, if you wish,' she said, silkily, and stepping to him, she laid a cool hand against his eyes, his mouth, his throat. 'You can come into my lands, but you are under a binding never to speak of it.'

'Never,' echoed Wat, fervently, his face fiery red. He glanced at Bertrand embarrassedly. 'Sorry, but it's what I've always wanted, as long as I can remember—'

'Oh, I know,' said Bertrand, many things making sense to him. Well, it was Wat's lookout. He had chosen it. He was quick and bright; he might cope well. And if he didn't . . . well, it was his life. Just as his own life . . . just as it meant that he knew that no matter what happened between himself and Tiphaine in the future, knowing her, loving her, had made him better and stronger and he would never forget it. Never. He looked at Tiphaine and she held his gaze for a long moment. And a great flood of happiness swept over them both; a happiness that knew it must be patient, that time alone, human time, would bring them as close as two human beings could ever be.

But Bubo was bored with love-looks. He turned to Viviane.

'As to you, Guardian, you can—'

'I will dispose of my own fate, thank you, Lord Bubo,' said Viviane, tartly.

'I never thought you would not, Guardian,' said Bubo crossly.

Rouanez laughed. 'You don't know her, Bubo!' she crowed. 'And I do. You can never win against such as her.'

'And neither can you,' snapped Bubo, but the humans had stopped listening to the korrigans' quarrels, being more interested in each other, and in their own gladness and relief at the prospect of going home at last, out of the hollow lands.

Epilogue

*T*ime the great healer did his work; and Tiphaine de Raguenel and her brother Gromer slowly learnt to be fully human again. You can imagine the joy of their parents, when they were returned; and the little manor, that had been so neglected for five years, lived again, full of laughter and quarrels, too, for being human means not always being at peace with each other. There was no more talk of sending the young people away to Court; the Viscount and Viscountess wanted to keep them close. Gromer was learning to run a manor, to understand it, and farming had turned out to be his great love. He was not the sort of lord who would ever leave his manor, but always love and cherish it, and the people who lived there. Raguenel would be in good hands. As to Tiphaine, she spent much of her time writing, and thinking, and reading, the image of future love warm against her breast, the reality of present love reknitting every fibre of her body and her *daouden*, which grew in power and beauty the older she grew.

Dame Viviane and Estik stayed with them for a year

or so; then the old lady said she was returning home in her turn, back to the great forest of Broceliande. Tiphaine knew she was seeking something of her own there: that her being had chimed with the korrigan-man who had so bravely put things right. She would go looking for Gwazig: and whether she would find him depended on whether he wanted to be found. Tiphaine often found her thoughts flying there, to that great green forest far away; to the old lady and the old bird, to the korrigan prince who had learnt the hardest way of all what made the real difference; and most of all to the young hedge-squire whose home was there.

One day, she knew, when her parents could bear it, she would go herself and find Bertrand; or he would come and find her. They did not write to each other, for Bertrand could not write or read. But she knew she could speak to him in her mind, and he would answer; it was one of the gifts the korrigans must have left with her, without saying: for if they do good, they do not like to be thanked, just remembered.

And she did remember. She would never forget what had happened, all of it, in the hollow lands. One day, she might be ready to catch sight of them again, the inhabitants of that strange, shifting Otherworld; but for the moment, she was content to remember.

As to Bertrand, his life had resumed its usual patterns: fighting, going home, fighting, going home. But everything had changed. He acted now with a bold lightness, an ease, a deftness, that none could ignore, and that soon caused him to come to the attention of those whose business it was to seek such talent. And so he was sought by the great ones of the King's Army, and asked to take on a detachment of troops, then another, and another. The day would come when he was the greatest soldier in all of Brittany and France, when the battles he would wage would help to turn the tide of a long and wearisome war. But he never thought of or imagined that day; the image that lived in his heart was that of the day when he would ride into Raguenel and see Tiphaine again, not just in his mind, but in reality. And then a flood of happiness would overwhelm him, and he knew he was blessed indeed, blessed in hope and love and beauty, greater by far than any battle-deed. Never once did he doubt her, in the years they were apart; for in the realms that humans call the hollow lands, strangely, he had learnt the hardest, simplest truth of all: that nothing can be well-founded, if is not built on absolute trust.

He too, often thought of the korrigans, and their strange countries, but without fear, for his experience had been different from Tiphaine's. He thought of his friend, Wat, and of Alain Mabig, and wondered how they were going, but heard no word.

Until one night, when he was riding back home to Broceliande, and coming around a bend in the forest path, he thought he saw, just vanishing ahead of him, three familiar figures, cloaked and wrapped, hurrying on mysterious errands: Gwazig, Alain, and Wat. He spurred his horse on after them, calling their names; but only Gwazig turned his head, and he heard only Gwazig's voice on the wind before the night swallowed all three up.

'He is well, Bertrand du Gwezklen; he is in his element, and so is the boy. Do not fear for them; think of them, but do not fear. Hold to your truth, Bertrand; and it will hold to you.'

'And what of you, Sieur Gwazig?' Bertrand called; but there was no reply. Only silence, and the night-sounds of the forest of Broceliande.

Afterword

This novel draws its inspiration from three main sources: Breton folklore about the korrigans, or fairies; the fourteenth-century English Arthurian story, Sir Gawain and the Loathly Lady (sometimes called Sir Gawain and Dame Ragnell); and the real-life story of one of Brittany's greatest couples, the poor-hedge squire turned brilliant knight and eventually commander of the army of the King of France during the Hundred Years' War, Bertrand du Guesclin (in Breton, 'du Gwezklen'), and his 'fairy' wife, Tiphaine de Raguenel.

Bertrand and Tiphaine were one of the most extra-ordinary couples of the fourteenth century: he was short, plain, very brave, intelligent and an extra-ordinary strategist; she was one of the time's greatest beauties, highly cultured, intelligent, courageous and reputedly with great psychic, or 'fairy' gifts, including the ability to foretell the future and communicate at a distance. Where she got these talents from, history does not explain, of course. But the story of their love is still remembered in the village of Raguenel; and

Bertrand and Tiphaine still live on in the collective memories of the people of France.

In the chronicles, it is mentioned that Tiphaine had a brother, but not what his name was. I have given him the name Gromer, the name given to the brother of Dame Ragnell in Sir Gawain and the Loathly Lady. In that story, Gromer and Ragnell have both been enchanted: Gromer as a kind of robot fighter-knight, Ragnell as a 'loathly', or very ugly, hag. The spell on them can only be lifted if the right answer to a question is found (in that story, the question is, 'What do women want?', and Gawain must find the answer).

Songs included in my story, such as that of Gwen'chlan, and The March of King Arthur, are real Breton songs which I've translated into English, as written down in the wonderful compendium of Breton songs, folklore, history and stories, the *Barzaz Breiz*, compiled in the nineteenth century by Breton folklorist Theodore Hersart de Villemarque. The story Tiphaine and Gromer read at the beginning, about the Wolf (representing France), the Bull (representing England) and the Ermine (representing Brittany), is a traditional Breton fable, also written down in the *Barzaz Breiz*.

I have also used other bits and pieces of Celtic folklore to create the world of the korrigans. The notion of a *daouden*, for instance, or 'doubleman' comes from an old Scottish Highlands belief that every human person has a doubleman, or visible soul, who walks along with them every day of their lives. This is documented in the extraordinary book by the Reverend Robert Kirk, *The Secret Commonwealth of Elves, Fauns and Fairies* (published in 1691). Other elements include Irish notions of the fairies particularly loving, and being

226

disarmed by, music and truth-telling. Most names for the korrigans and other characters are taken from Breton folklore, except that of the korrigan lord, Archduke Bubo, whose name and presence is borrowed from the biggest European owl, the eagle owl, known as 'hibou archiduc', or 'archduke owl' in French, and 'Bubo bubo' in Latin. The korrigan names for things, such as *mabrokorr* for their world, and *mabroden* for the world of humans, and the word *daouden* itself, I made up using combinations of Breton words.

Though the Hundred Years' War was a time of turmoil, suffering and danger in France, medieval wars were not 'total' wars, in that often they consisted of skirmishes followed by long periods of quiet. Alliances often shifted over the period – for instance, some Bretons were allied to the cause of France, others to that of England, still others refused to ally themselves to anyone and harassed troops of both camps. So some unlikely friendships were formed. In fact, quite often, bands of supposedly 'enemy' soldiers would join together (mostly, it has to be said, for looting).

THE TEMPESTUOUS VOYAGE OF HOPEWELL SHAKESPEARE

Sophie Masson

Hopewell Shakespeare is spellbound by the Globe theatre, where the plays of distant kinsman, William, fire his fantasies of love and fortune. Craving adventure, he joins the crew of a notorious buccaneer hunting for the legendary Lost Island of the Lord of Alchemists, where all dreams come true.

But on the journey of his life, Hopewell finds that dreams and nightmares can be very close together . . .

Another Hodder Children's book

CARABAS

Sophie Masson

They hated her. She knew that. She could see it in their eyes, their twisted faces.

When the people of her village discover Catou's unusual gifts, she is banished forever with only Frederic, the miller's son, as company.

But now she is free to follow her true nature, to turn her gifts to her advantage. Before long, she and Frederic had found their path into the opulent Court of Tenebran, to its strange powers, its mysteries and its terrifying challenges . . .

'Masson's narrative is resplendent with surges of lyricism.' *Reading Time*

'A captivating narrator . . . who knows how to hypnotize her readers.' *Lollipops*

'A sophisticated and timeless tale of magic and human nature.' *Weekend Australian*

CLEMENTINE

Sophie Masson

There is something I must tell you. The romantic secret of it has burned brightly in me, the dream thrilled in every pore of my skin. So bear with me, and come with me, into a place long ago and far away . . .

Aurora, daughter of the Count of Bois-Joli, and Clementine, the woodcutter's child, have been friends for sixteen years. Until, one day, they stumble on a castle they never knew existed . . .

A century later, Lord Arthur, a young scientist, feels himself strangely drawn into the legend of the sleeping castle of Bois-Joli, and finds that science is no match for a magic that has lain untouched for over a hundred years . . .

'an elegant fantasy romance full of delicious eighteenth-century detail and an exquisite French setting.' *The Times*

'the detail of court life and ways is enthralling. A fabulous novel . . .' Adele Geras, *TES*